ARE WE NUTS?

A MODERN FABLE

GISELA HAUSMANN

Educ-Easy Books • Greenville, SC

Book layout by www.ebooklaunch.com
ISBN 978-1-7324211-1-0
Library of Congress Control Number: 2018906505

We will be known forever by the tracks we leave.
– Dakota Proverb

CONTENTS

Wiki Scroll

From Wikipawdia, the free encyclopedia

Sciurus States

Map

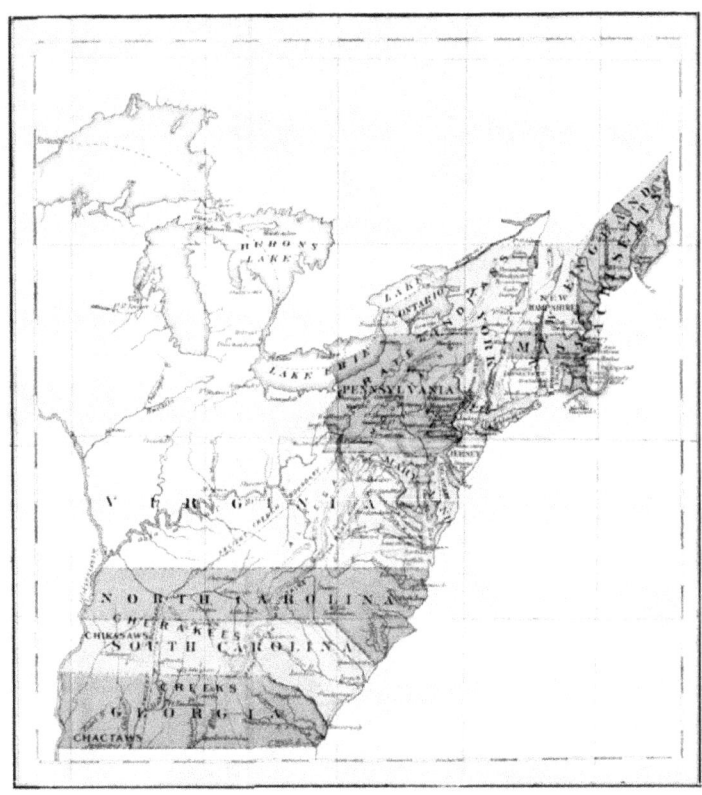

Flag

Coat of Arms

Motto

"In Squirrelity We Trust"

Anthem

"Everybody loves a Nut"

Capital

Nuttington

Ethnic groups

Members of the family Sciuridae
40.5% gray squirrels
25.3% red squirrels
11.4% tan squirrels
7.7% flying squirrels
5.4 black squirrels
4.9% white squirrels
4.8% orange squirrels

Government

Federal presidential constitutional republic

Legislature

The Tribe Council

Area
• Total
177,776 sq mi

Population
• census
175,641

Currency

Pistachio gold nugget

INTRODUCTION

"How did we get this information?" A rather corpulent gray squirrel turned away from a smartphone screen and looked irritated at the six squirrels who attended the secret meeting.

Christopher Bitsquirrel who had called the meeting cleared his throat. "Bob Smitcorn sent a private kuk from somewhere in the west, perhaps Nutchez. I expected follow-up kuks but we haven't heard from him or the other team members. Here is a fact sheet for everybody." He handed out the six small scrolls that lay next to him.

The room fell silent as the squirrels studied the summary. Finally, the tallest squirrel let out a resigned laugh. Then he declared in a threatening voice, "Gentlemen. This information cannot leave this room. If it does, our plans are doomed." All squirrels nodded, including Christopher Bitsquirrel with an uneasy expression.

After a minute, a thin-lipped squirrel began drumming with his paw on the edge of the wooden table. Then, he said slowly, "About this information – do we even know if it is true?"

He stroked his whiskers thoughtfully. "Maybe this information is not real but an exaggerated doomsday forecast? At this point we really can't be sure because Bob Smitcorn did not send any follow-up information."

The corpulent gray squirrel immediately embraced the idea. "You are right! We do not have conclusive evidence yet." Almost all squirrels seemed baffled at this statement.

Still, a white and a gray squirrel wanted to agree with their leaders and shouted, "Hear, hear." Then, feeling all eyes on him, a modest red squirrel uttered, "Having more information would certainly help." Only Christopher Bitsquirrel never even nodded, let alone agreed aloud. He was thinking, "But what if Bob Smitcorn is dead?"

"Gentlemen! Pleeease!" the tall squirrel called the others to order. He briefly examined the facial expression of each attendee. Then, he stated with gravitas, "Gentlemen, let us call a nut a nut. It would be inconvenient if this information were true. We are planning to launch an economic revolution next year. Our interests – the interests of the republic – are at stake. Therefore, I believe it would be irresponsible to share this information with the tribe as long as we are not one-hundred percent certain that it is correct."

"Exactly! Irresponsible!" the thin-lipped squirrel agreed.

"Haste makes waste," the white squirrel offered.

"Look before you leap," one of the gray squirrels concurred.

Smiling satisfied, the corpulent squirrel got up from his hay pillow. "Okay. Since we all agree, I propose to wait with any further action until we get more facts. Christopher, please notify us immediately when you hear from Bob Smitcorn. Meeting adjourned."

1 – HARRY

(Eighteen months later…)

It was an extraordinary day. Harry just knew it. The obvious proof was – he had spotted a big, juicy raspberry. Raspberries were so rare, he had only seen them in pictures.

His view of the raspberry bush was partially obstructed by an oak tree he had wanted to climb. Then again, he had already forgotten the oak tree, the acorns, and everything else.

Stepping closer, Harry saw that the raspberry bush had produced only a single berry.

Even better! This meant it was his.

If the bush had produced more than one berry, he'd be required to run back to the burrow, report the finding, and get help with harvesting the sweets. The bounty would be shared by many squirrels. Who knew if he'd be allowed to eat a whole berry? No food gatherer he knew had ever found a raspberry.

There was but one conclusion to be drawn. Better eat the raspberry before another squirrel came by.

Cautiously, Harry climbed the thorny cane, secured the berry with a spider web thread, and carefully lowered it onto a big flat rock right underneath. Then, he jumped down to savor the treat. Slowly, he munched each drupelet separately. *Oh my... What a delicacy!*

Harry laid back on the sunny rock and reflected on how lucky he was. In school, he learned about the devastating catastrophes the squirrel society had to endure after the Great Disastrous Floods.

Though there had been signs and forewarnings, the disastrous surge had arrived suddenly. Tens of thousands of huge trees on which squirrels built their nests got felled by funnel winds and millions of squirrels were killed. Woods and farmlands, and most of the squirrels' nut depots, got destroyed. As a result, millions more squirrels slowly starved to death.

After the waters receded, the fathers of today's nation, George Squirrelton and Benjamin Franknut, told his great-great-great-great-great-grandfather's generation that the squirrels had to organize themselves to form a society that helped all squirrels in all of the land.

The wisest of the squirrels came together and laid down the rules, for instance, that squirrels could eat a single berry if they found one. Although the guidelines allowed for small indulgences, in general, all decrees focused on securing the health and safety of all squirrels, nationwide.

Still, conditions stayed grim for a long time. The tribes had to move often because excessive heat and storms destroyed their food supply. His own mother died during one of those devastating storm periods.

Things only changed when the late, great Steve I'Squirrel discovered that the weird boxes they found in deserted human dwellings could be used to communicate with other tribes. I'Squirrel named them smartboxes. And clever Bill Gatsquirrel discovered an industrial complex full of power kernels which stored the magic power that kept the smartboxes working. A school was set up so squirrels could learn using the boxes.

Then, President Bill Clintsquirrel, who embraced all new technologies, promised a smartbox in every classroom in the nation. Legend had it that it took the efforts of more than ten thousand squirrels to distribute the thousands of smartboxes and power kernels to all tribes in all the lands. Luckily, he, Harry, became a beneficiary of this program.

The clever idea led to great prosperity in the squirrel nation.

The year after the boxes were delivered, the *Brighter Future for Squirrels* Conference was held for the first time. Steve I'Squirrel and Bill Gatsquirrel were the keynote speakers. They explained how using the newly discovered technologies would help squirrels in taking control of their future.

Harry remembered the event well. Using the smartboxes, I'Squirrel's and Gatsquirrel's comments were live streamed to most squirrel tribes. It was the first time that squirrels saw moving pictures.

Soon thereafter, legendary Jeff Bizsquirrel set up a trading platform. Tribes who needed healthy foods could order them by using the smartboxes. And Bill Russellsquir, Bill Waddellsquir, and Alex Majorsquir set up a transport system to deliver foods and goods to all burrows in the entire republic. They named their company *The Deer Express*.

The inventive trio accomplished this seemingly impossible task by setting up partnerships with deer societies. The deer transported squirrel messengers and merchandise in exchange for vital information about the weather, storm damage to woods and fields, updates about the water quality of rivers and lakes, and, of course, predator sightings.

To protect the nation and support their allies such as the deer societies, The Squirrel Council also established the Central Kernel Agency for the specific purpose of collecting, analyzing, and disseminating this kind of relevant information.

Somewhere behind Harry, a branch cracked.

Startled, he sat up and looked around. "Better hide," he thought. A deer broke out of the woods and ran downhill. Even though he could only glance at it, Harry spotted Phillip Deerrel, his tribe's finest messenger, on the back of the deer. Obviously, Phillip returned from making a delivery.

"Phillip is going to climb the career ladder," Harry thought. "And I? I have been daydreaming, again. If I keep doing this, The Council will never give me permission to go on an expedition."

Going on an expedition was his ultimate goal. He would have gladly traded the raspberry or even a dozen, if he had that many, just to get permission to go. Alas, the bitter truth was that The Council had turned down his request with the words "not this year," for the second year in a row. There was no arguing with The Council.

Harry decided to return to the burrow and record the coordinates of the raspberry bush. If, in the future, it'd produce plenty of fruit, maybe he would get promoted; after all, he discovered the bush. And maybe, a promotion would lead to getting permission to go on an expedition.

2 – NUTTINGTON

Located in the Appalachian Mountains, Nuttington, capital of the Sciurus States, was literally a shining city upon a hill.

The gray squirrels' main burrow was a state-of-the-art compound. Tunneled below a 250-year-old oak tree, it offered amenities unheard of in the world of squirrels. Ever since the discovery of the smartboxes eliminated the need to relocate, the tribe invested in creating the infrastructure to support their society's ambitious way of living.

Most remarkable was the Nuttateria, where squirrels could dine on nuts, fungi, seeds, dried insects, and caterpillars, and even small bird eggs. Located at the center of the burrow, the Nuttateria served as a living monument of the squirrel nation's greatest accomplishment – overcoming the hardships of the past, the famines that killed more than ten million squirrels nationwide.

There was also a government center where the president and The Council worked, a business center where squirrel industrialists discussed new ideas and deals, a scroll library with a scriptorium, two dozen community warehouses that stored nuts and other edibles, and more than one hundred suites for influential squirrel families and important guests. At the backside of the burrow, next to a lake with a pine chips beach, *Nuttington Bowl* hosted concerts and plays. On event days, the adjoining beach bar even served artisan pecan liquor.

A pleasant walk away, in the valley to the north, next to a human-made cell tower, the burrow's tech hub had been established. The campus included the Smartbox Center, the school, the academy, a training center, and a burrow with suites for teachers and visiting squirrel lecturers.

To the east of this subdivision with the lofty name "Brainhub," half a dozen sweet potato fields stretched through the valley, also serving as an outdoor lab for the school's agriculture program. North of the *Squirrel Academy* entrepreneurial squirrels had set up artisan workshop-burrows. There, they produced maize scroll sheets, woven nut baskets, straw pillows and mattresses, gourd water containers, and other luxury items their grandparents had not even dreamed about.

Returning to the main burrow's Biz Center, Harry pulled his file to note the exact location of the raspberry bush and mark its coordinates on a map made from maize husks.

This idea – to record and collect the food gatherers' data – was the cornerstone of the Sciurus States' success, even long before Steve I'Squirrel discovered the smartboxes. Mapping out their secret hunting grounds helped the squirrels in streamlining the harvest-to-storage process.

While Harry double-checked that his delicious information was properly recorded Cassandra Keela Allsquirrel lined up behind him. Cassandra Keela, a geeky-looking Northern Flying Squirrel, had moved here from Virginia. Most everybody called her Cee-Kee.

"Hey Harry, good to see you," she said. "Did you already visit your Great-Grandpa? I heard he was looking for you."

"Thanks, Cee-Kee." Harry dropped the quill and rushed through the tunnel system to the back of the burrow. Because Great-Grandpa was the tribe's oldest member, he lived in a suite deep underground where it was warmer during the winter.

3 – JUANITA

"Great-Grandpa, guess what I found." Harry dashed into the living room, then stopped in utter surprise. Next to Great-Grandpa sat a young, black squirrel girl he had never seen before. The girl had the biggest, prettiest eyes but her dark fur was matted and uncombed.

"Who are you?"

"Now, now, Harry, please don't forget your manners." Great-Grandpa smiled mildly. "This is Juanita Squirnández. Originally, her family lived in a region called Texas. Apparently, Texas is a country in the southwest of the continent. During the Great Disastrous Floods, their tribe's life raft log was swept east, and they built a new life some-where southwest of here, on a barrier island. Unfortunately, a few full moons ago, her tribe's burrow got flooded during a big storm and most of the tribe members perished."

Great-Grandpa briefly glanced at Juanita to see if his telling her story upset her, but she did not blink an eye. He continued. "The few

9

survivors tried to find a new tribe. Juanita got separated from her friends, but the clever girl was able to hitch rides on a few deer. The deer brought her here – to Nuttington."

Wow, what a story. Harry gasped. He loved hearing adventure stories. Turning to Juanita he asked, "How many moons were you traveling? By the way, I am Harry. Pleased to meet you."

Surprised at his reaction, Juanita stammered, "Many moons... many, many moons. Along the way I tried to stay with a few tribes but they did not want me." She looked a bit embarrassed. "They called me a black rat with a bushy tail."

How strange. Harry bit his lip; he didn't know what to say. Squirrels' furs came in all colors – gray, tan, red, orange, blonde, black, and even white. Why had these squirrels called Juanita names?

"Now, girl, there is no need to cry." Great-Grandpa smiled at her. "You can stay with us. We think your dark fur is very pretty."

And, turning to Harry, he said, "Why don't you show Juanita around and introduce her to the tribe? It's time for my afternoon nap."

4 – FREEDOM, EQUALITY, JUSTICE, & SQUIRRELITY

Back in the tunnel system Harry asked Juanita, "So, what would you like to see first?"

"Oh, I don't know, I have never visited a big burrow like this one. I am hungry. Could I maybe get some nuts before we look at anything?"

"Sure. We have a Nuttateria. Please follow me."

The Nuttateria had been tunneled right under the big oak tree. Juanita could see the exposed tap root at the back wall. It was decorated with a carved wood portrait depicting George Squirrelton and Benjamin Franknut. But since Juanita knew nothing about the founders of the Sciurus States, she did not recognize them.

Speechless, she stared at the neat arrangement of hazelnuts, hickory nuts, pecans, pine nuts, and walnuts that were stockpiled by variety and size along one of the walls. On a root that served as a counter stood small pine-bark dishes filled with wild cabbage pieces and dried caterpillars. At the very end of the counter sat a couple of gourds labeled "water." Juanita had never seen anything like this eatery.

Two Nuttateria attendants appeared and greeted them happily. "Hey, Harry, what's up? And who is your friend?"

Harry smiled back and replied, "Thanks for asking. Why don't you give us a sample basket? Guys, this is Juanita. She is from the southwest. We don't know what kind of nuts grow there. So, it's probably best if she samples a few of ours."

Then, turning to Juanita, he suggested, "Let's eat outside. It's a beautiful afternoon."

He ushered the bewildered squirrel girl through the backdoor. A few minutes later, they sat down on a moss pillow between the oak tree's surface roots. Juanita eagerly grabbed a pecan and nibbled on it.

"Thank you. This is so good. I was so hungry. I haven't eaten anything all day."

"You are welcome, Juanita. Didn't you have a Nuttateria at your old home? I thought all burrows had one."

"Our old shelter was nothing like yours. I've never even heard the word Nuttateria, let alone seen one."

For a second, she looked as if she was about to start crying.

"Originally, like really long ago, my ancestors lived in a wildlife refuge, in Texas. Then, the Big Disastrous Floods came."

She sniffled. "Since the oldest and wisest squirrels in the refuge had forecasted the catastrophe for a long time, we were ready, but we did not expect to be swept to a totally different region. When my ancestors' life raft log landed on that barrier island, my family and their friends didn't know how to survive in a sandy environment without trees. Still, it was a blessing in disguise because nobody could migrate to the island. All the food was ours.

"I was born on this island. Then, some moons ago, another storm passed right over our tribe's burrow. Four of us managed to get on a wooden board that floated by and made it to the mainland. The rest you already know."

As she recalled the tragedies in her life, Juanita looked forlorn, but Harry was impressed with her and her story. In his opinion, Juanita was a real explorer, like the legendary Amelia Squirhart. Hopefully, he could get her to tell him about her ride on the wooden board once she had settled in.

"Well, Juanita, welcome to the Squirrel Republic's capital. It's a very advanced burrow. We even have a trading platform that allows us to acquire non-native nuts, seeds, and even intelligence scrolls from all states of the Union. Not all communities are connected but most mid-sized and all larger burrows are."

"States? Republic? What's that?" Juanita was obviously confused.

Only now Harry realized that Juanita could not possibly know anything about the Sciurus States. She had lived on an island. "Sorry, Juanita. I should have explained.

"After the Great Disastrous Floods struck, influencers George Squirrelton and Benjamin Franknut realized that if we squirrels didn't work together, we might not survive. Of course, at the time, when whole valleys were under water, and trees and burrows were covered with disgusting green slime, things were pretty difficult. We could not reach all squirrels on the continent. So, thirteen states on the East Coast formed a republic – the Sciurus States. Since then, a few other states have joined this Union. All squirrels who live in the Sciurus States help each other."

"Oh, wow," replied Juanita, who was still unsure what exactly a republic was. "I am sorry. I never heard of the Sciurus States. And, what's a trading platform?

"Our trading platform? Oh, you'll love it. It's really cool!" Harry beamed with pride. "Basically, it means we can get anything we want. Anything!"

He leaned back against the tree and made himself comfortable.

"Remember, after the Great Disastrous Floods struck, the humans disappeared. Supposedly, there are still a few of them around but nobody from this tribe has seen a live human in generations. Of course, when they disappeared, they left stuff behind; most importantly, the smartboxes.

"It took a few generations but then the late, great Steve I'Squirrel figured out that squirrels could use the boxes to communicate with squirrels living in other burrows and even in other states. This breakthrough changed all our lives. Instead of having to send messengers, we can broadcast information using the smartboxes. Tragically, Steve I'Squirrel passed away too soon but his pal Mike I'Nut teaches advanced courses right here, at our burrow's academy."

Harry paused for effect.

"It's been very good for us. We use the smartboxes to trade with many other tribes and we haven't experienced a famine since I was little."

Harry's new friend was impressed. Though she could not imagine how this trading platform worked, obviously, it was an amazing system. It had to be. The mere sight of the Nuttateria filled with the most delicious treats said it all.

"Is this what you do, Harry? Trading with other tribes? Can I learn it too?"

Harry laughed. "You'll probably have to go to school. There is much to learn. And you'll have to live by the Sciurus States' laws. Our squirrel society's creed goes as follows." He stood up, put his paw over his heart, and recited:

"I believe in the Sciurus States, as a government of the squirrels, by the squirrels, and for the squirrels; established upon principles of freedom, equality, justice, and squirrelity."

Sitting down again, he explained, "Basically, it means that all of us are equal and that all of us work together. In a good year, most adult squirrels can stockpile 3,000 to 10,000 nuts and seeds, depending on size. Whereas in the olden days some of this effort was lost because squirrels forgot the locations of their hiding spots, today we manage to have a surplus, every year… or, almost every year. Consequently, when squirrel influencers Steve I'Squirrel and Bill Gatsquirrel discovered that we could use the smartboxes to exchange information, we began trading with other tribes."

"Business greats Jeff Bizsquirrel and the founders of the Deer Express established the infrastructure. Jeff Bizsquirrel set up the smartbox platform where we offer our goods to other tribes. Naturally, they offer their merchandise too and that's how we trade. And the Deer Express delivers the goods. Didn't Great-Grandpa say that a few of the deer gave you a lift?"

Juanita nodded. "Aha, so that's how they knew where to drop me off?"

"Exactly. Also, a few years ago, influencer Bill Gatsquirrel set up a foundation to reduce extreme poverty. His foundation donates nuts to poor tribes so their societies don't stay behind."

Harry stopped his excited monologue for a second.

"Why don't I show you how it's done? The Smartbox Center is next to this tall tower over there." He pointed at the cell tower in the valley, about 2,000 squirrel jumps from the mighty oak tree.

Juanita could only nod. Her head was buzzing, and she was wondering if she would be able to remember everything she heard, especially the names of the squirrel greats.

5 – THE SMARTBOX

The Smartbox Center turned out to be a human-made building right next to the cell tower that could be seen from everywhere in the neighborhood. It was veiled with a façade system of white rods that cast shadow onto the building. On its flat roof, strange looking blue, reflective panels pointed toward the sky. Three squirrels stood guard in front of its wide-open door. Nearby, three others were sitting in the shadow of a big monument sign that read Technology Solutions.

"Who is with you, Harry?" one of the guards demanded to know.

"Juanita Squirnández. She is a refugee. Great-Grandpa told me to show her around."

"Oh, well, then it's okay."

"Your Great-Grandpa must be a really important squirrel," Juanita guessed aloud, as they entered the bunker.

"Yes, he is." Harry smiled proudly. "Great-Grandpa is a direct descendent of President Theo Roosquirrel.

"Theo Roosquirrel was the youngest squirrel president in history and one of our greatest leaders. He pushed The Council to pass the Nut Inspection Act, and he also made nature conservation a squirrel issue."

"Wow!" Though Juanita was confused by many of the things she heard, she began wondering if, maybe, just maybe, her life was taking a turn for the better. Apparently, these squirrels had everything a squirrel could wish for, and then some.

As they walked deeper into the bunker, Juanita could see a big, well-lit room at the end of the hallway. A second later, the smartbox came into view. The flat unit lay in the middle of the floor. It glistened, almost magically. Though it was about the length of a squirrel tail, Juanita judged that she would be able to lift and carry it because the smartbox was very slim. She thought, "Aha, so that's why the building is so heavily guarded. So nobody can steal the precious box." Her thoughts were interrupted by loud shouting.

"Hey guys, how are you? How can we help?" Two squirrels who stood amidst piles of scrolls on a human-made table, in a corner of the room, tried to get Harry's and Juanita's attention.

"Oh, it's you, Harry." Both squirrels jumped down from the table.

Harry greeted them. "All good, thanks for asking. This is Juanita Squirnández. She is a refugee who is moving in with Great-Grandpa and me. I am just showing her the box. She's never seen one.

"Juanita, meet Christopher Bitsquirrel and Fred Bytesquirrel. They are two of our tribe's most excellent smartbox experts."

Politely, Christopher and Fred greeted Juanita a second time, but she didn't seem to hear them. Juanita stared at the see-through top of the smartbox, mesmerized.

Through the glass she could see tasty-looking, striped sunflower seeds, black symbols beside them, and a few golden stars. She remembered that she had not seen sunflower seeds in a long time and wanted to touch them. But, before she could stretch out her arm, Harry put his paw on the glass. The sunflower seeds disappeared; instead, dark-shelled hickory nuts popped up. Next to these nuts were also black symbols and golden stars.

Juanita gasped. Where did the sunflower seeds go? And how come this slim box could hold big, juicy hickory nuts as well? They did not even fit into the box.

Just as she wanted to ask how this magic worked, two other squirrels entered the room. Harry looked up.

"Hi there. Sorry for the interruption. We are already out of here."

He pulled on his friend's arm and whispered, "Juanita, we've got to go. We did not have an appointment. This space is reserved for business and research."

As they left the bunker, Juanita noticed a complicated system of wheels and hemp ropes next to the inside of the entrance door. But finding out what this thing was all about would have to wait. She was more interested in finding out how the magical smartbox worked.

6 – THE FOOD GATHERING EXPEDITION PROGRAM

Once outside the building, Juanita couldn't hold back any longer.

"Harry, how did the sunflower seeds and the hickory nuts get inside the smartbox? Why are there golden stars? And what are the black symbols for?

"Good questions!" Harry laughed. "The nuts and seeds aren't in the smartbox, only their pictures.

"Christopher and Fred aren't the only technicians at the Smart Box Center. In an adjoining room, skilled squirrel technicians take pictures of the nuts and seeds we want to trade. Other technicians upload these pictures to the trading platform. Then, they add descriptions of the seeds' size, quality, and other pertinent info, for example, if we were able to get this type of seed to sprout. This information is contained in what you call the black symbols. We call them letters. Squirrels learn to read and write letters in school.

"As soon as the pictures and the descriptions are uploaded, squirrels all over the nation can see them on their smartboxes. If other tribes like our goods, they can trade with us. And, once they receive the merchandise, they can rate it with golden stars. Five stars is good and one star is bad."

Juanita listened, spellbound. *So, this was why Nuttington's squirrels were so successful – they figured out how to create maximum profit!*

Of course, her experiences on the island were not relevant as the island where she grew up was not an ideal habitat for squirrels. But she had heard stories about the way her ancestors lived in the Texas refuge. Before the Great Floods arrived, there was always enough food for everyone to eat, and that's what her ancestors did. That was all her ancestors did – they ate nuts.

In contrast, Nuttington's squirrels collected nuts, ate some, stored some, and traded others. They also planted nuts – deliberately – to grow more trees. That's why they could afford to donate nuts to poor tribes in the republic. The way it looked, Nuttington's tribe did not simply live a good life like her ancestors did; they discovered the secret to infinite growth in the post-disastrous world. She, Juanita, wanted to learn how this system worked.

"Wow, Harry! Can I watch the smartbox technicians do all of that?"

"Yep. If you go to squirrel school, you'll be taken on a guided tour and you'll learn how to use a smartbox.

"At Nuttington burrow, we have seven smartboxes available for the public, to be used for research or business. One at the school, three at the academy, one at the smartbox center, and two at the library.

"At the academy, you can also take advanced courses to become a smartbox technology expert like Christopher and Fred. But I'd advise you against it. The technology experts work inside all day. They never get to run around in the woods. That's why I enrolled in the Food Gathering Expedition Program."

Juanita tried to wrap her head around these totally new concepts. Apparently, she needed to get a job if she wanted to stay at Nuttington burrow. But getting a job would not be easy. Every time she asked if she could do this or that Harry said she first needed to go to school.

Harry, who was obviously proud of his tribe's achievements, kept on going. "We also have other outdoor jobs." He pointed to the east.

"Over there, about eight hundred squirrel jumps away, is the center of our *Foods for Squirrels* project. Visionary George Squirrel Carver planted the first sweet potato plants there. Squirrel farmers continue these efforts as well as experiment with trying to grow other seeds.

"Following President Theo Roosquirrel's plans, we also plant tree seeds to prepare for the future. One hundred thirty-seven of them have grown into bigger trees and sixty-one of these trees have produced record harvests. Additionally, entrepreneur squirrels run their own nut plantations.

"Unfortunately, this year was not a good year, especially farther west. The region has experienced frequent storms during the last six months and we had to send quite a few emergency rations. Still, we have been able to cover the difference with nuts we stored last year."

"Wow," Juanita thought out loud. "On the island we never really got a chance to do anything like this... Harry, you seem to know everything. Are you an influencer?"

As soon as she said it, another thought crossed her mind. What if she did not have the skills to live with this tribe? What if they did not want her to stay once they figured out how inept she was?

Harry didn't seem to notice that she became all quiet. All of a sudden, he looked neither happy nor proud.

Somberly, he said, "I wish I was an influencer, but I am not. Please don't tell anybody but sometimes I feel like a failure. Squirrelgod in heavens, I am a descendant of Theo Roosquirrel, yet I am still a food gatherer. Not really at the bottom of the food chain but still... you know what I mean."

Juanita, who didn't know what a food chain was, nodded anyway and Harry spilled his guts.

"I wanted to be an explorer so badly. My father was a pathfinder, but that was before we began using smartboxes. So, after I passed school with flying colors, I enrolled in the Food Gathering Expedition Program at the academy. In my mind, I saw my team and me going on expeditions, discovering new lands, finding amazing new nuts and fruits, and bringing back their seeds. I wanted to be an explorer whose name would be mentioned on history scrolls."

"What are scrolls?"

"Scrolls are made from corn husks. We use them to record important information including what our influencers thought and taught. This way, no knowledge is getting lost."

Juanita shook her head in sheer astoundment, then she refocused. "So, how have you failed?"

Harry took a deep breath. "I wanted to follow in my father's footsteps, maybe even become an explorer like squirrel great William Clarksquirrel. But that's not what happened – or at least not so far. Even though I did well at the academy, I did not graduate at the top of the class. Bob Smitcorn was the nuttidictorian."

He grinned, embarrassed.

"So, in the Spring of last year, when the Tribe Council chose the leader of the first expedition to explore new territories in the west, they picked Bob Smitcorn, not me. His team members were Tom Davinut and Sue Millwood. Then, the real problem happened. They – Team 1 – were supposed to return six full moons later, but they didn't. They also stopped sending messages four moon cycles after they left. It's been more than a year since we heard from them."

Juanita whispered, "Oh, no," but Harry didn't even hear it. He kept venting his frustrations.

"Naturally, the tribe and The Council fear that all three may have died. As soon as we learned that Team 1 had disappeared, Team 2, consisting of Sean O'Squirrel, Paul Bugsquirrel, and myself, offered to embark on a rescue mission but – The Council declined. Shortly thereafter, they put the entire program on hold. Great-Grandpa says, "That's so typical.""

Aping somebody Juanita did not know, Harry orated in a deep voice, "Imagine a descendent of Theo Roosquirrel dying from heatstroke, in a land far away…"

He laughed, slightly sarcastic. "Great-Grandpa is not concerned. I asked him. He has no problem with me exploring new worlds and finding new foods. But, he says, I need to figure it out for myself."

7 – INFLUENCERS

A bit frazzled, Juanita tried to grasp the entirety of this complex situation. Evidently, living in this wealthy republic looked easier than it actually was. Here, squirrels had to compete to be able to do the jobs they had trained for. Even worse, apparently, sometimes, squirrels did not get to do what they had learned at all.

"Can't your dad help you? I mean, if he is a pathfinder he should have some influence."

"No, unfortunately, that's not possible. My dad died. Both my parents died. Mom during the last famine, when I was little, and dad never returned from his last expedition." Harry sniffled. "The crazy thing was, my dad left at the onset of the last famine, trying to find food. Since he and his team did not return, the misery got only worse. Then, mom died three full moon cycles later."

Juanita gently hugged Harry's shoulder. "I am so sorry. I know how you feel. After my friends and I made it to the mainland, I thought I should have never gotten on that wooden board but instead searched for my family."

Before Harry could answer, he and Juanita heard loud shouting. Two squirrel girls appeared on the small hill to the southeast. "Grassroots meeting. Everybody – the grassroots meeting is about to start."

Spotting Harry and Juanita they came running. "Hey, Harry, are you going to attend? With your friend?"

"Not today, ladies. Juanita just arrived."

Harry hugged the girls and made the introductions. Annie and Emma Speednut were founding members of the grassroots organization *YoungNutcrackers*. Not surprisingly, they wanted to recruit Juanita as soon as they heard that Great-Grandpa had invited her to stay. Totally dedicated to their cause, they left only after Juanita promised to attend next week's meeting.

Juanita was excited. She loved the word "grassroots movements." It sounded like something she could relate to. "Harry, what exactly does a grassroots movement do?"

"*YoungNutcrackers* is a grassroots movement of young squirrels working on getting *our* voices heard. Many of us feel that The Tribe Council doesn't address the concerns of young squirrels, specifically the students' tuition costs.

"See – the smartbox revolution created a demand for high-tech jobs. We also need more farming experts; after all, everybody needs to be fed. However, the academy is so expensive that it causes problems for the students. I know it first paw. Since the Explorer program was put on hold, Sean and I have to work jobs we did not choose just to pay off our loans. Other young squirrels don't even try to enroll in the academy."

"*Rancid peanut!*" Juanita thought. Apparently, acquiring an education was more difficult than she guessed. "But how can I go to school then?"

"Sorry, Juanita, I explained it all wrong. Basic school is free just like basic food. Attending the academy is expensive just like ordering fancy foods or goods on our trading platform."

"What can the grassroots movement do about it?"

"We organize meetings and try to work with The Council so the council members represent our interests too, not only the interests of the Bignuts-50. The truth is – the tribe needs us. Who is supposed to do the work in the future?"

8 – THE BEST ROOM EVER

Realizing that he was introducing more and more concepts Juanita did not know, Harry interrupted himself. He did not want to scare her by making things sound too complicated. Maybe it was best to change the subject.

"Want to go for a quick bite? I don't have too much time, though. Tomorrow I need to get up really early. Since it rained yesterday, my best friend Sean O'Squirrel and I need to harvest wild mushrooms. The best time is in the early morning, before deer could trample the sprouts accidentally."

"Can I come along and help you with harvesting wild mushrooms?"

"Sorry, that's not an option. The burrow's rules explicitly state that only trained members of the Food Gathering Expedition Program are allowed to harvest wild mushrooms. We learned to distinguish between good and poisonous mushrooms at the academy. Sean is a graduate too."

Remembering some of the pranks Sean and he had pulled during their school days, Harry giggled spontaneously. "You'll like Sean. He is my best friend. By the way, Sean has different fur, too. His is reddish golden. He is a descendent of an Irish line of squirrels who moved here from Bostonut burrow."

Before Harry could continue telling Juanita more about Sean and their enduring friendship, Juanita interrupted him. "Harry, is it okay if I lay down? I am really tired. Today, I saw more new things than I knew existed."

"Right. I am sorry. You must have had a rough day. Let's go. I am sure you can sleep in our suite, there is plenty of room for three."

As they walked back through the tunnels, Juanita noticed another unusual thing. The tunnel's walls were covered with dried straw that was plastered against the loam.

❖

Great-Grandpa was already waiting for them. "So, Juanita, how d'you like Nuttington?"

"Thank you, Great-Grandpa. It's an amazing burrow, or better – an amazing world. Harry showed me so many new things that I am totally wiped out."

"Yes, yes, I thought so. I put out a new hay mattress in the guest room."

"Thank you very much," whispered Juanita. "Today was my best day in many moons."

As soon as she said it, Harry thought of the raspberry. He had to tell Great-Grandpa. But first, he wanted to make sure that Juanita was tucked away. He really wanted Great-Grandpa to be the first to hear about the raspberry. After all, Great-Grandpa was his only family.

With an elegant gesture he guided Juanita to a cozy chamber, separate from the other spaces he and Great-Grandpa called their rooms. A fresh hay mattress lay on the floor. Next to it stood a leaf plate with dried worms and a hollow chestnut filled with water.

Juanita got dreamy eyes. "Oh wow, this is the best room I ever slept in."

"Well, then good-night," said Harry and rushed off to Great-Grandpa's room.

9 – GREAT-GRANDPA

"Sooo?" inquired Great-Grandpa. "What'd you find today?" For a squirrel his age he had a mighty excited undertone.

Harry grinned. That was just like Great-Grandpa. Great-Grandpa really cared about him. And about exciting stuff.

"You did not forget," he said with a big smile. Then, he whispered in his ear, "I found a raspberry. A ripe, juicy raspberry. And – I ate it."

Great-Grandpa's eyes widened. He whispered back, "A raspberry? Holy Pistachio! I did not expect that. This is big." He closed his eyes, thinking about the unusual development. "You know, Harry, I believe finding a raspberry is a sign. Something big is about to happen.

"In my long life, I only found two raspberries and each time something big happened. The first time, President John F. Kennesquirrel got elected. What a charismatic leader he was. I am sure you have heard his famous quote, 'Ask not what other squirrels can do for you, ask what you can do for other squirrels.' And three days after I found the second raspberry, Steve I'Squirrel introduced the smartbox. Steve said, 'It's a breakthrough squirrelnet communicator.' And, indeed, it was."

"That's amazing." Harry leaned back on his hay pillow. "So, what do you think might happen this time?"

"Oh, I don't know. Then, the squirrels didn't believe that Kennesquirrel could get elected and they also did not think that I'Squirrel's work could result in a revolutionary breakthrough that would affect all our lives. If something is going to happen, it might be an event of equal magnitude. We can only wait and see… And now – shouldn't you be going to bed?"

"Yes, I probably should." Harry got up. "How else will I be rested enough to accomplish the big things I want to do?" He pounded his chest and laughed. "One never knows… After all, I found a raspberry today."

As he was leaving, Harry turned around and said, "Just so you know, I didn't tell anybody about the raspberry, not even Juanita. It's our secret. Good night."

Great-Grandpa did not get up from his hay pillow. He just sat there and smiled. Though he had never pondered the thought, he suddenly realized that he had been waiting for this moment. He wondered why he had forgotten about finding his two raspberries. Each time he found one, he felt so special. Harry could use a boost. Since The Council grounded the Explorer program, Harry had been restless and disappointed. Finding the raspberry might encourage him to look for new goals.

10 – "OUR SMARTBOX WORLD"

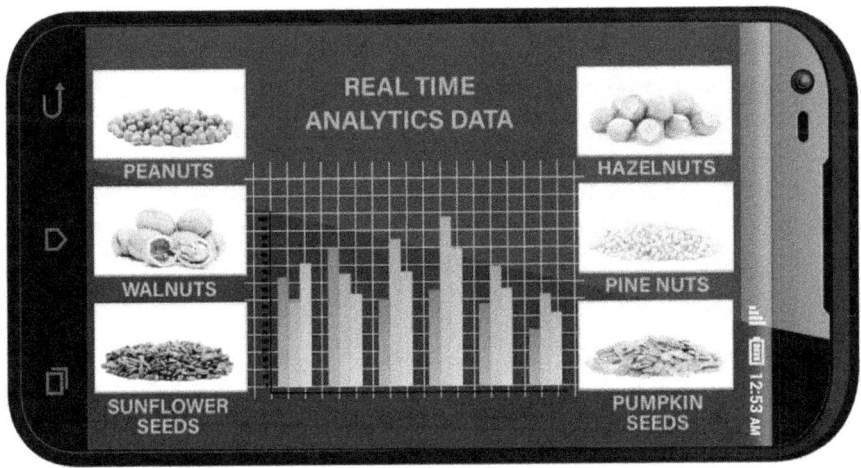

The following day Juanita awoke late. It was quiet in the burrow. Probably all squirrels were out and about doing interesting things, she thought.

She inspected her fur and tried combing it. That didn't help much. Regardless of the angle she looked from, her fur looked matted and noticeably thin, which was even more obvious because her fur was black. She was sure the problem was caused by malnutrition; after all, she had been homeless for quite some time.

Turning this way and that way to inspect her tail, Juanita suddenly noticed the plate with dried worms next to her mattress. Didn't mom always say that worms are high protein, low carb, and paleo friendly?

Quickly, she ate all the worms off the plate. What next? Harry was out harvesting mushrooms. Should she just walk over to Great-Grandpa's room? She cleared her throat purposefully.

"Good morning, Juanita," Great-Grandpa called from the next room. "Do come in. How do you feel?"

"Somewhat overwhelmed, in a good way, like a naive country squirrel who's arrived in the big city."

Great-Grandpa roared with laughter. "Juanita, if I may offer a word of advice – don't be so impressed.

"Yes, our society achieved successes once deemed impossible but not every facet of life became better. Unfortunately, some things became more difficult. Personally, I miss our squirrel Can-Do spirit.

"During the years of hardship, squirrels welcomed and celebrated every new idea that might help improve our lives. In contrast, today, everything seems to be about feasibility studies and marketability. Many ideas fall through the cracks."

Though she did not know what feasibility studies were, Juanita nodded. "Yes, Harry told me that The Council won't let him go on his expedition."

Great-Grandpa shook his head. Then he stated with deliberation, "Well, of course, Harry could go. He could go rogue. But that's not what he wants. Harry wants to be an official explorer instead of a rebel explorer."

"Why does The Council even care? That's what I don't understand," wondered Juanita. "If you were worried and if you told him not to go, I'd understand. You are his Great-Grandpa. To The Council he is just another squirrel even if you guys are descendants of the great Theo Roosquirrel. Harry says The Council worries about the explorers' safety. I don't believe that. Squirrels die, every day, like my own family died. When the tribe started the explorer program, they must have known that exploring new lands is dangerous."

Great-Grandpa looked impressed.

"Well, well." He chuckled. "You are probably right. Here is the catch: The explorer teams take a smartbox along so they can communicate with us and record information. Personally, I believe, the entire

Food Gathering Expedition Program is not so much about 'Food' as about 'Gathering' – meaning the gathering of all kinds of information.

"Did Harry tell you that Team 1 disappeared? They had a smartbox with them. Maybe I am wrong, but I believe The Council and our famous Central Kernel Agency fears that other tribes may have found the box and may be trying to use it. And that's why they grounded the program. They don't want to risk other squirrel tribes outside the republic getting access to the smartboxes."

"Oh, peanut! What was I thinking? I should have figured out this one." Juanita groaned.

"Well, Juanita, welcome to our smartbox world. This is how the smartboxes changed our lives. Some of us worry more about the boxes than about squirrels. And some of us worry more about marketability and investment returns than about boldness of vision."

Great-Grandpa took a sip of water from his chestnut cup.

"For instance – see this cup? Frank Lloyd Wrillel invented it. He also designed this burrow."

"Uh-oh," Juanita chimed in. "I saw some of his inventions. The tunnels' walls are plastered with straw."

"Exactly. Frank invented this technique on his own. He was quite a squirrel… Frank also designed the straw bag beds and even these cups. That was before analyst geek squirrels, acorn investors, and venture nuttists ran feasibility studies for even the smallest projects."

Great-Grandpa snorted in anger. "I am not so sure that this new way of doing things is best for the tribe. I believe The Council and the acorn investors should fund and support unrestrained creativity because, by golly, most of them don't come up with anything new."

He exhaled with frustration. "However, what concerns me the most is – The Council and the analyst squirrels are in charge of all data. We don't actually know what they do with it. What if they interpret the data incorrectly?"

He sighed once more and then smiled at Juanita. "Enough of the heavy talk. Do you want to go to school? You don't have to go if you don't want to."

"Oh, yes, I'd like to learn about the smartboxes and the pictures of the sunflower seeds inside the smartbox…"

"Splendid. Let's take my shortcut to school. My secret pathway isn't nicely trampled as the main path, but it's a heck of a bit shorter. Which is what matters to an old squirrel like me."

11 – LOCK-DOWN

Stepping out of the burrow, Great-Grandpa pointed down into the valley where the cell tower overtopped even the highest trees. "See the tower down there? From here you cannot see the building next to it because it's hidden by trees. That's where the Brainhub is located. And the school and all educational facilities. However, instead of taking the main road to the Hub, we'll walk over the ridge to your left."

Pointing at the ridge, Great-Grandpa continued, "In part, it's a steep path but it's not a bad path. A few years ago, we planted Table Mountain pines there. Table Mountain pines are particularly profitable trees. Their seeds remain viable for ten or more years. That's why squirrels aren't allowed to run through the grove so they don't disturb the saplings. I have permission to cut through because with age comes privilege." Great-Grandpa grinned. "Follow me. This trail offers one of the prettiest panoramic views in all of Nuttington."

They hadn't walked two-hundred paces when the Smartbox Center came into view. The building seemed to be on lock-down. All six guards stood at attention in front of the building. The main door that had been wide open the day before was closed. Today, the place looked like a fortress.

Juanita glanced at Great-Grandpa. He had stopped walking. Ducking behind a boulder on the ridge, he gently pushed her down as well. Together, they peeked over the rock. Whereas Juanita was mostly curious, Great-Grandpa felt a deep uneasiness. This show of force was alarming. Did they expect an attack?

The shadow of the pine branch above Great-Grandpa's head moved about the length of two pine needles when finally, the Smartbox Center's door opened. Out came two squirrels. As soon as they walked through the door, somebody inside the building closed it.

"Holy Pistachio! That's secretary Chip Gagwood and council squirrel Dick Hushsquirrel," whispered Great-Grandpa. He felt even more uneasy. Clearly, the guards were guarding what was going on inside the center, not what might possibly happen outside.

Chip Gagwood and Dick Hushsquirrel took the main road that led to the main burrow. As they were walking, they stopped twice and seemed to argue but Great-Grandpa and Juanita could not hear what they were saying. Finally, the two legislators disappeared behind a group of young maples. Great-Grandpa sank down behind the boulder.

"The tall one was secretary Gagwood, the other council squirrel Hushsquirrel. For sure they did not visit the center to take classes," Great-Grandpa snorted sarcastically.

"What does this mean?"

"I have no idea what they were doing there, but they don't pay cordial visits."

"So, what are you going to do?"

"Watch and observe. For the moment, that's all we can do."

Great-Grandpa closed his eyes for a minute and Juanita waited quietly. Much to her surprise she heard him whisper, "It's the raspberry event."

"Sorry?"

"Nothing, Juanita, nothing. I was just thinking out loud. Listen, why don't you skip school today? Harry can take you tomorrow."

On their way back to the main burrow Juanita walked as slowly as possible so Great-Grandpa could keep up with her easily, on the steep, rocky path. It gave her time to inspect the young Table Mountain pines.

She marveled at the tribe's accomplishments. By the time the next generation of squirrels grew up, the pines would offer shade and protection from the wind, hinder erosion, and produce hundreds of seed cones to feed the squirrels.

12 – A FIRST PICNIC

Meanwhile, Great-Grandpa pondered the strange event.

Over the last few years, life in the Sciurus States had improved immensely, mainly because of the smartboxes' vast effect on communication and business. Today, squirrel tribes could warn each other about approaching severe weather. Tribes whose harvest grounds got affected by extreme weather events were no longer isolated. They could ask for help in the form of emergency rations as well as volunteers who helped them to rebuild.

Also, generating economic forecasts for the following years became a piece of nut. These days, with the help of the smartbox' calculator app, analyst squirrels were able to generate the harvest reports and the forecasts within only ten days.

Which left a lot of time for designing other applications.

Certainly, squirrels had a natural propensity toward gathering stuff – some squirrels more than others. Which was why Great-Grandpa believed that certain power squirrels had moved on from gathering nuts and seeds to gathering data with the intent to use this information to their advantage.

That's why he was irritated seeing the Smartbox Center on lockdown. It seemed to confirm all his suspicions about clandestine activities taking place within its walls.

As Great-Grandpa and Juanita neared the grove's exit, they spotted Harry sitting on a boulder chatting with a red squirrel. Juanita noticed that that the red squirrel had ear tufts just like she did. She guessed that this was Harry's best friend Sean O'Squirrel.

After making introductions, Harry told Great-Grandpa and Juanita how he and Sean learned where to find them.

"Cee-Kee told us. When Sean and I returned from harvesting the mushrooms, we met her at the storage room. She told us that you and Juanita were visiting the pine plantation. Cee-Kee always knows everything. Yesterday, she also told me that you…"

Harry interrupted himself and seemed to consider what he was about to say. Finally, he asked, "Great-Grandpa, it is kind of strange that Cee-Kee always knows where you are, isn't it?"

"Yes, it is. Say – do you boys want to have a picnic dinner in the grove?"

"YES!" Harry and Sean high-fived each other. "We'll get everything. You and Juanita go ahead and make yourselves comfortable. We'll run to the Nuttateria and pick up dinner."

Watching them run off, Juanita noticed how close the main burrow was and asked, "Great-Grandpa, aren't you worried that Cee-Kee will see us?"

"Ha!" Great-Grandpa laughed. "Apparently, Cee-Kee watches me wherever I go, here or elsewhere. But Cee-Kee can't enter the grove unless a senior squirrel accompanies her. She may be watching us, but she'll have to do it from a distance. We'll be eating here because I want to tell the boys what we saw."

"Do you know why Cee-Kee watches you?"

"No." Great-Grandpa scratched his ears. "But I am much more irritated about the Smartbox Center's door being closed. You see, the guards are posted to protect visitors in the event that a fox or a coyote comes by. Which begs for the question, why double the number of guards when the door is closed? If the door is closed, predators can't enter the center. By the way, we don't have secrets from Sean. He is a trustworthy young squirrel and Harry's best friend."

As if his words were a cue, Harry and Sean came running down the path carrying a nut basket. Harry also pulled a gourd. They were still laughing when they arrived. "Okay, let's eat," exclaimed Harry and placed the basket together with the gourd in the center, within everyone' reach.

Great-Grandpa took a pecan, bit off and then probed, "Did you boys notice anything strange going on at the Smartbox Center? Did you hear about any problems?"

"We didn't go there today because we were out harvesting mushrooms. Why?"

With a concerned voice, Great-Grandpa elaborated on what Juanita and he had seen.

"Hmm," said Sean, "I thought the Smartbox Center is only closed at night."

"Actually," said Harry, "the center opens one hour after sunrise and closes when the smartbox technicians assess that it's getting too dark."

Great-Grandpa barely listened. Just as he could tell if a nut was rancid merely by looking at it, he knew that the closed door signaled some kind of trouble. Eventually, he pondered out loud, "Well, well, all of this is very interesting, indeed. For the first time ever, the Smartbox Center's door is closed during the day. The guards seem to be on high alert, code red or orange, or whatever code. Our government officials visit the Smartbox Center, and somewhat surprisingly, I am being watched by Cee-Kee Allsquirrel. What do we make of that?"

The squirrel boys were silent and, as it was his habit, Great-Grandpa scratched his ears.

Juanita coughed briefly and said, "I think it means that The Council is doing things other than calculating the harvest results."

Great-Grandpa seemed momentarily stunned, then he laughed and clapped his paws. "Nicely done. Juanita summed it up in one sentence. Maybe you boys should venture out of Nuttington every now and then and learn to deal with new challenges?"

Harry and Sean were abashed. Clearly, Juanita, who had been homeless after surviving a natural disaster, possessed field smarts and she was not afraid to say her piece. Finally, Sean piped up. "But The Council won't give us permission to go on our expedition."

"I can't go rogue. What would that do to our lineage?" Harry added.

"What about our lineage?" Great-Grandpa questioned. "Granted, Theo Roosquirrel came from an excellent squirrel family, but he built his legacy himself. Theo lived on the frontier; he was an exceptional nut gatherer, he became the youngest president in the history of the republic and…" Great-Grandpa raised his voice and his paw, "Theo fought The Council of his days to get the Nut Inspection Act passed. Theo didn't listen to The Council; he made The Council listen to him."

Smiling briefly, Great-Grandpa closed by saying, "Theo Roosquirrel believed with all his heart that a single squirrel's actions could have an effect on the course of big affairs… And that's how he lived his life."

Stunned, the three squirrel youngsters gaped at Great-Grandpa, with open mouths. He grimaced. "Ok, kids. End of rant. I just meant to say that we shouldn't be complacent. No, I don't know what's going on at the Smartbox Center but I can tell *when* something is going on. Also, I don't like it when I am being watched.

"And now, let's all go to bed and sleep on it."

13 – "HE TOLD BILL"

Meanwhile, in another part of Nuttington, a squirrel messenger was rushing through the burrow's tunnels, knocking on the doors of five apartments and delivering a memo scroll to each of the residents.

Not even half an hour later, the five recipients met for an emergency meeting in a conference room two floors below the Nuttateria. Mitchell Tallsquir was already waiting there.

Visibly upset, he began the debate without greeting the others. "We are facing a new problem. Christopher informed Bill." Tallsquir's eyes sparkled with anger.

"What did he tell Bill? About the kuk?" the white squirrel tried to verify.

"No, not that! Christopher told Bill Gatsquirrel about the problem with the power kernels."

Tallsquir dabbed his forehead with a small grass towel. Then, he continued.

"Apparently, the Smartbox Center's best practices protocol demands that Bill must be informed of all hardware problems. I did not know that. Also, I thought that by advising the Central Kernel Agency to classify this problem as top-secret, we had it contained.

"However, as all of us know, when Christopher discovered the issue, Bill was out-of-burrow, in Port Evernut. And because the Central Kernel Agency classified the power kernel problem as top-secret, Christopher could not send Bill a private kuk.

"But while I thought we put the issue to rest, Christopher, that nit-picker, follows protocol and informs Bill as soon as he returns – in person! Worst of all, he did not even tell me. I found out about all of this when Bill Gatsquirrel stormed into my office and told me he'll be leaving for Virginia as soon as the sun rises tomorrow morning. Bill believes there might be another warehouse full of power kernels in Virginia."

"*Really?* So, what are you upset about? It seems Bill is going to solve *our* problem." The white squirrel smiled relaxed.

"I too think this is excellent!" The corpulent squirrel grinned. "Now we don't have to worry. Bill will solve our problem but use his resources. Let the private sector deal with as many inconveniences as possible."

Mitchell Tallsquir sighed and dabbed his forehead again with his grass towel. Then, he said sternly, "That is a careless view of things. Obviously, the more squirrels know about problems the sooner things will unravel. That's why I told the Central Kernel Agency to classify the problem as top-secret.

"What if some of the tribe members wonder why we need a huge supply of power kernels? What if some of them start asking questions?"

The corpulent squirrel got up from his straw bag chair and said, "Mitchell, you are overreacting.

"Nobody is going to find out anything. If you feel it's necessary, create a diversion. Write a press release about the upcoming economic revolution. Speak to that reporter, Sean Limsquirrel, and ask him to quaa our message. Or throw a parade. And now: Can I invite you all to a late-night macadamia nuts dinner?"

14 – GARY LOGISQUIR

The next morning, Juanita, Harry, and Great-Grandpa got up early. Juanita was still combing her fur when she heard Harry say, "Please, hurry up, Juanita. The best seats in the Nuttateria go quickly."

He was right. The Nuttateria was buzzing with activity. A good three dozen squirrels were sitting at the tables, eating and chatting away; others were waiting in line at the counter. Three squirrel children were jumping up and down impatiently with their mothers trying to calm them. Juanita had never seen so many squirrels in one room.

Harry only glanced at the crowded room and made a quick decision. "Great-Grandpa, why don't you and Juanita grab a table and I'll get the food."

Trying not to stare at everybody, Juanita followed Great-Grandpa to a log table in the far corner. Close by sat a group of squirrel teens munching away on walnuts and listening to one squirrel who read out loud from a scroll. Juanita was wondering if they were students and if she'd see them again at school.

As soon as Great-Grandpa sat down, an energetic-looking, white squirrel with elegant demeanor approached the Roosquirrels' table, patted Great-Grandpa on the shoulder and teased, "Well, good morning! I am chuffed to bits. Aren't you up early?"

Then he bowed to Juanita and said, "Miss Juanita Squirnández, I presume. Mademoiselle, your arrival is the talk of the burrow."

Great-Grandpa roared with laughter. "Juanita, don't believe everything my friend Gary Logisquir says. He has a flair for the dramatic. Also – beware if he invites you to play nut-checkers. Gary is Nuttington's number one player who represents this burrow in the state championships. We play every other weekend, and he wins nine-and-a-half out of ten games."

Turning to Gary Logisquir he said, "Look who is up early himself! Gary, if indeed, Miss Squirnández is the talk of the burrow, it's for a good reason. She possesses the important talent of thinking logically and drawing conclusions."

Gary Logisquir bowed again to Juanita. "Charmed and delighted. Now I hope even more that you'll give me the honor of playing nut-checkers with me, sometime soon. Will you be attending this month's 'Friday Lake Night' party? I hope to see all of you there. Unfortunately, I must leave now. I take tai-chi classes in the morning."

Not a minute after he left, Harry arrived balancing a tray loaded with food and drinks. "Squash salad and chilled dandelion water," he announced as he placed the tray on the log table.

"Superb. I love the smell of squash in the morning," declared Great-Grandpa.

While they were eating, Juanita wondered what her parents would say if they could see this amazing eatery, eat these fabulous foods, and meet interesting squirrels like Great-Grandpa and Gary Logisquir. Eventually, her ponderings were interrupted when Great-Grandpa asked, "Harry, will you walk Juanita to school?"

"Absolutely!" replied Harry with a mischievous grin. "It's a perfect opportunity to take a closer look at the Smartbox Center. Maybe, I can find out something. After I drop off Juanita, I'll meet up with Sean and we'll be checking the sweet potato fields. Unfortunately, the Biz Office assigned us to check if the students overlooked spuds and also to dig up any remainders."

"Well, you kids have a wonderful day. I am planning to visit the library. If you can't find me, just ask Cee-Kee."

The two squirrel teens laughed, got up, and went to the exit. There, they waved good-bye and started walking toward the Brainhub subdivision.

15 – SQUIRREL SCHOOL

As Harry and Juanita approached the Smartbox Center, everything looked as it always did. Only three guards stood in front of the door which was wide open; the second crew was eating breakfast on the grass patch in front of the monument sign.

Harry cursed under his breath, "There goes my plan. If the door isn't closed, I can't ask why it is closed." Juanita who heard it was stunned by how driven he was. Harry seemed to be on a mission at all times.

Arriving at the school, Harry and Juanita saw a group of students playing nut-ball on the burrow's front lawn. Of course, Harry ignored them. Juanita assumed that he was busy working out scenarios that would prompt the guards to talk.

At this early hour, the squirrel school's big classroom was still empty. Juanita looked around. On the far side of the room stood two hollow log chests filled with corn husk sheets. The log chests also supported a good dozen straw pillows that were stacked neatly between them. Right above the pillows hung a poster featuring beautiful drawings of many kinds of nuts, some she had eaten before and others she did not recognize. Juanita noticed that the letters N-U-T appeared next to almost all illustrations.

Hanging on the wall to her right was a poster that showed a fox, a coyote, and a raccoon, each accompanied by illustrations of their respective paw prints and tracks. The poster on the left wall displayed pictures of a hawk, an owl, and an eagle. The three flying predators were depicted in two different kinds of poses – mid-flight as well as sitting on a branch.

Juanita who had never seen educational materials was fascinated. On the barrier island, she and her friends had to figure out everything for themselves. Sadly, squirrels who didn't learn quickly enough often got killed. Turning around, she noticed a big black panel. Somebody had drawn white symbols on this panel. "Letters," Juanita thought and said,

"Wow, Harry, your school is so cool," to which Harry replied, "Just wait till you meet Mr. Khansquirrel. He is the super coolest teacher you can imagine."

When Mr. Khansquirrel finally arrived, Juanita was dumbstruck.

Her new teacher had dark fur, not as dark as hers, but almost as dark. She, Juanita, was not the only dark squirrel living at this gray squirrel burrow. Best of all – dark-furred Mr. Khansquirrel was a teacher, a respected member of the community.

Confidently, she introduced herself, "Good morning, Mr. Khansquirrel. I am Juanita Squirnández. I am ready to learn."

16 – A WHISPERING GUARD

Happy that the wait was over, Harry uttered a quick, "Have fun, y'all," and hurried back to the Smartbox Center. As luck had it, one of the guards whistled as he got closer.

Harry knew that asking fact-finding questions was probably not a good idea. Most likely, the guard would clam up. So, he casually strolled to the building and teased, "Ghee, you guys have such an easy job. You just stand here all day whereas Sean and I have to do the dirty work. We are supposed to check on the sweet potatoes. That is hard work."

Then, he laughed slightly cynically, hoping that the guard would fall for it. Promptly, he did.

"Harry, you have no clue," the guard replied. "We work hard too. Yesterday, the center was inspected by secretary Gagwood and council squirrel Hushsquirrel. Instead of having to handle the heavy door pulleys only once in the morning, we had to do it four times. Open – close. Open – close. It's a top security procedure!" The guard raised his eyebrows to underscore the significance of the event.

"Really? That's new," Harry empathized. "And – did you pass?"

"Oh, this wasn't about us. We guards are good. Christopher Bitsquirrel and Fred Bytesquirrel held a presentation. I heard them mention the word 'mapping.'"

"What kind of 'mapping?'"

"Oh, I don't know, we guards were outside. I was wondering why only secretary Gagwood and council squirrel Hushsquirrel attended. That was kind of unusual. Typically, when the guys do a presentation for The Council, many more members show up."

"Hmm, I hope there isn't a problem."

Still trying to bolster the importance of his job, the guard mouthed quietly, "They didn't look too happy." Then, he stated in a confident, loud tone, "It's going to be okay. They did not issue an order or anything."

Harry knew he wasn't going to get more information from this guard. Checking the sun's position he noted, "Ouch, I am already late. The potatoes and the dirt are waiting. Be watchful. Byyye."

17 – SEAN O'SQUIRREL

By the time Harry arrived at the fields, Sean was waiting there. Hearing the latest news, he agreed that the fact that the guard felt a need to whisper was at least somewhat suspicious. "So, what do we want to do?" he asked.

"Great-Grandpa thinks there is a problem," Harry replied, "and Great-Grandpa is a wise squirrel."

He thought of the raspberry and what Great-Grandpa had told him about finding a raspberry. "I think we should investigate what's going on. For sure nobody is going to tell us anything because nobody ever does."

With an annoyed expression, Harry scanned the potato field.

"Just think about it… Is this what we want to do for the rest of our lives? Auditing agriculture students' work? Is this what we went to the academy for? And why we worked our tails off in the strenuous Food Gathering Expedition Program?"

Harry grinned. "I'll tell you something, Sean. We try to come up with a plan to get inside the Smartbox Center – undetected. If we can come up with a plan, we go for it, and if we don't, we don't. We have plenty of time to think about it while we work."

Each of the six potato fields was approximately three hundred squirrel jumps long and one hundred jumps wide. Since the agriculture students had already worked the fields, the originally neat rows of plants were in disarray; piles of dirt and holes were everywhere. To make matters worse, dried potato plant vines, which the students left behind, were lying around everywhere.

Performing a follow-up check was going to be a time-consuming task. Still, the Biz Office had requested the audit because a comparison of harvest results indicated that this year's sweet potato harvest was below last year's by approximately thirty percent.

Now it was Harry's and Sean's job to find out if this was a case of underperforming students or an unexpectedly bad harvest. Harry, who hated digging for tubers, thought that the only good news was that it rained only once in the last three weeks. Dry soil made it much easier to check for remaining spuds.

While digging in the dirt, Harry and Sean both pondered the strange events of the last forty-eight hours.

Sean wondered if Harry was blowing things out of proportion. Was there *really* a reason for concern? Maybe Harry just wanted to compensate for not being able to go on his expedition. Regardless, he, Sean, would support Harry because Harry was his best, if not his only friend.

Sean's family had moved to Nuttington when he was still a pup. At Nuttington's school, he was the only redfur in his class. Though nobody teased him about his fur, Sean's classmates liked to call him an egghead. In a way, they were right. Whereas they spent most of their free time playing and talking about nut-ball, he, Sean, preferred reading technical scrolls and tinkering with gadgets.

The only other squirrel boy in his class who also did not appreciate nutball was Harry. That's how they became best friends. Harry liked to read adventurers' story scrolls; together, the boys reenacted most of the stories.

On many afternoons, they hiked through the woods pretending to be legendary explorers William Clarksquirrel and Meriwether Lewinut. They also jumped around in trees pretending to be Amelia Squirhart and Fred Noonut. It was so much fun Sean never minded that Harry always played famous Amelia Squirhart and he always had to play Fred Noonut, whose name few squirrel students remembered.

If making friends was hard when he was only a pup, it became even more difficult once he moved on to the academy. Everybody was always busy and everybody was always overwhelmed by all they had to do. Sean knew older students who felt isolated. Hence, when Harry enrolled in the Food Gathering Expedition program, Sean joined Harry even though he would have liked to take mechanical engineering classes.

Sean felt best friends should stick together. Also, Harry told him that his construction skills would come in handy if they needed to build a pine bark raft while on expedition in the frontier lands. Now that there weren't going to be any expeditions, why not engage in solving this mystery?

18 – A FAILED LEGACY

Meanwhile, Harry wondered how they could find out what was going on behind the Smartbox Center's closed doors. Ever since The Council had turned down his request to lead a search and rescue mission trying to find Team 1, Harry had lost trust and confidence in The Council's desire to address unexpected problems. In Harry's mind, the council members were trying to keep the status quo and avoid challenges.

Harry also knew that other squirrels had similar thoughts. That's why Annie and Emma Speednut founded the *YoungNutcrackers*. If Sean and he could not solve the mystery of the Smartbox Center by themselves, maybe they needed to involve the *YoungNutcrackers*, or at least a few of them.

Still, the biggest problem was that there was no glaring problem. It was all guesses and hunches.

Naturally, Harry trusted Great-Grandpa's intuition. As the oldest member of the tribe, Great-Grandpa had survived every conceivable catastrophe from famines, countless relocations, to predator attacks. Even Gary Logisquir liked to point out that Great-Grandpa had amazing instincts; otherwise, he would have died a long time ago. Like his grandson – Harry's father.

Harry swallowed hard, picked up a potato plant vine, and threw it as far away as he could. In his heart, he knew that even though his father had failed, for sure, he had done his best. But other tribe members hadn't seen his father's efforts in the same light.

When Harry was still a young pup, by chance, he overheard Buddy Slugsquirrel say that it was irresponsible of Great-Grandpa to allow Harry's father to go on an expedition "when he should have stayed at the burrow" at the onset of the last famine. Slugsquirrel had implied that Harry's father's mission was doomed from the beginning and that therefore his Great-Grandpa made the wrong decision.

Harry never told Great-Grandpa that he heard what Buddy Slugsquirrel had said. It did not matter. Because, sooner or later, he himself would redeem his father's failed legacy.

Was this *"the moment"*?

Harry didn't know but he hoped that finding the raspberry was a positive omen.

19 – MAGGIE CARNEGIESQUIR

After the kids left for school, Great-Grandpa headed to the library. Still a sprightly squirrel, he had a plan of his own.

Located at the back of the burrow, the library consisted of the scroll room, the media room, the study room, and an adjacent scriptorium which was closed to the public. As a rare exception, the library contained human-made elements. During the construction of the burrow, the squirrels hauled three aluminum sorting trays into the space and placed them upright to serve as scroll shelves. To anchor them in the chamber, they used the humans' nails and screws that had been stored in one of the trays. Frank Lloyd Wrillel, the architect, was quite proud of this ingenious idea. The scroll shelves allowed easy access to the educational materials and also protected the scrolls during heavy downpours.

Maggie Carnegiesquir, granddaughter of Andrew Carnegiesquir, who founded this and many other squirrel libraries, was the head librarian. She asked visitors if they wanted to use one of the two smartboxes or read scrolls and helped with finding materials, if needed. Maggie Carnegiesquir also scheduled the calendar and made sure that the library visitors did not abuse their guest privileges. However, she never asked Great-Grandpa any probing questions. Her grandfather Andrew Carnegiesquir and Theo Roosquirrel had been casual acquaintances.

"Hello Maggie, a glorious day to you," Great-Grandpa greeted her. "Is it okay if I check the *Smart Kuks&Quaas* on a smartbox?"

"And the same to you," Maggie answered with a tiny, flirtatious smile. "Just go ahead. I expect this to be a quiet morning."

Great-Grandpa really preferred reading the *Nuttington Weekly Gazette* of which twenty copies were hand printed and made available at the library, every weekend. However, since the next *Gazette* would be released only in two days, on this day his only option was to check the latest news on the smartbox.

The *Smart Kuks&Quaas* was not a fancy site like the trading platform; it featured only text but no pictures. Influencer squirrels could add their own news, in postings of 140 characters or less.

Once alone in the media room, Great-Grandpa inspected the smartbox because he hadn't used one in a long time. Finally, he typed "#Nuttington" into the search field and pressed the enter button. Having lived through what sometimes seemed like 1,000 years of hardship, he never failed to be impressed with "stuff just popping up" on the smartbox's screen. Great-Grandpa found the ease with which things happened on the smartbox spellbinding, and also a bit threatening.

As always, the *Nuttington Kuks&Quaas* reflected the buzzing burrow's range of events and activities.

> #nuttington #weather advisory. high temps persist. expect evening rain. food gathering expedition team scheduled to harvest mushrooms

#nuttington messenger Phillip Deerrel delivers emergency ration. 4 bags #blackwalnut @ #salemnutterry

refugee Juanita Squirnández from texas and southern barrier island arrives via deer express @ #nuttington

#august #fullmoon: well known artist Andy Warhazel will exhibit painting series #Campbells nut soup cans at #nuttington Nuttateria

#nuttington bushy tailers nutball season schedule to be published on #harvestmoon day

#nuttington nutball hall of famer michael Jordacorn commits to visiting @ next year youths summer camp and work with pup campers

#nuttington bowl: actors Richard Burtnut & Liz Taylmond will perform celebrated off-nutway play 'whos afraid of a wolf' on supermoon day

#nuttington Nuttateria adds dried crickets to menu

#nuttington #weather advisory. unusually high temps persist. 110/84

Great-Grandpa sighed and shook his head. These kuks did not contain the information he was looking for. Maybe he wasn't doing it right? He could ask Maggie for help but then she'd find out what he was doing. Maggie was a clever squirrel lady, and she was also really good at putting two and two together.

Great-Grandpa scratched his ears. Suddenly, he remembered what he learned during the smartbox training: "You can use different hashtags to search the same topic." He pondered the thought for a minute and then typed the word "#smartbox" into the search field.

FOXEYE! – the newly displayed kuk-quaas announced:

register to learn new #smartbox skills. #ecommerce #cryptonuts. explore additional #investing and #training opportunities #richnutville coming soon. #smartbox #ecommerce training #brand #brand-design #raleinut

#smartbox #ecommerce training. #cryptonuts business solutions. Coming soon to your burrow

#smartbox #smallbusiness #entrepreneur #ecommerce #nut-hacking #digitalnut #pittsburrow

coming soon to a location near you. #smartbox #cryptonuts #ecommerce training #success

And more than fifty similar kuk-quaas he didn't even want to read.

Great-Grandpa was stunned. These kuk-quaas presented a puzzle. Why had he never heard about this ecommerce stuff?

Then again, not one kuk-quaa indicated anything about a problem. All kuk-quaas sounded upbeat and excited. What did it mean? That there was no problem or that whatever was going on inside the Smartbox Center was a total secret?

While he was pondering these questions, Maggie Carnegiesquir peeked through the doorway, quite unexpectedly.

"How much longer d'you need the smartbox, d'you think?" she probed, in the kindest of all ways.

"Oh, I am done, Maggie. Thank you as always." Great-Grandpa smiled and quickly closed the browser window. "Are you expecting visitors who need to access the box?"

"No, but I have been asked to limit visitors' usage of the smartboxes. The other day, Christopher Bitsquirrel told me that he and Fred Bytesquirrel are performing some kind of maintenance operation. In all honesty, I did not fully understand what they were doing. He used so many complicated words."

Great-Grandpa's eyes lit up. As casually as possible, he asked, "Any problems?"

"I don't think so," Maggie replied. "But I know that Christopher Bitsquirrel told Mr. Khansquirrel the same thing." Noticing Great-

Grandpa's interest, Maggie added, "If you want, I can send you a messenger when this maintenance thing is over."

"Thank you for your gracious offer, Maggie, but that's not necessary. In fact, I would be grateful if you don't mention that I was here. You see, I was just trying to… I was only taking a peek, a refresher if you so want."

Maggie Carnegiesquir wrinkled her forehead but Great-Grandpa, who didn't want anybody to find out what he was doing, had his little white lie ready.

"Maggie, you may have heard that Harry and I have a guest staying with us – Juanita Squirnández?"

"Oh, yes, yes. The refugee girl. The poor thing. I heard she lost all her family and all her friends." Maggie Carnegiesquir's voice trembled with compassion.

"Yes, sadly so. Of course, Harry is explaining all our fancy technology stuff to her. As for me – I just don't want to look like an over-the-hill squirrel. So, I wanted to check if I still know how all this works."

Maggie burst out in a short, refreshing laughter, the kind of laughter that would have prompted her to hiss "tsk-tsk" at any patron who would have dared to laugh out loud inside her library.

"Your secret is safe with me." She smiled and bent her head slightly towards Great-Grandpa.

And he who thought very highly of Maggie thought, "Probably, all secrets are safe with you, Maggie, but are you aware of the secret activities that go on behind the closed door of the Smartbox Center?"

Out loud, Great-Grandpa said, "I kiss your hand, Maggie. As always, it's been a pleasure visiting you. Would you fancy joining Harry and me for a picnic sometime? You'd also meet Juanita."

"That sounds lovely."

"Splendid! I'll send Harry when we decide on a date. A tender adieu."

Leaving the library, Great-Grandpa decided he needed to climb the

Big Oak, not all the way, but up to the second level branches. Maybe, sitting up there and looking at the grand scheme of the burrow, he'd have a bright idea, or reach some clarity.

20 – A PLAN

It was almost lunchtime when Harry wiped the sweat off his forehead and started to grin. Right this moment he wasn't even bothered by the heat and the dust, because he just had a fantastic idea, striking in its simplicity.

"Sean – break time!" he hollered out loud, just in case somebody was watching them. Then he walked over to the hole in the ground where Sean had placed their provisions.

As soon as Sean joined him, he whispered excitedly, "Sean, I just remembered something. I think it could be important.

"The day before yesterday, I took Juanita to the Smartbox Center. I just wanted to show her the box. This was the day before Great-Grandpa saw the door closed.

"When we entered the main room, I saw Christopher Bitsquirrel and Fred Bytesquirrel on the human-made table in the corner. They had stacks of scrolls up there, and they were doing something with them. I was busy showing Juanita things and didn't pay attention to what they were doing. But now, I am wondering.

"In all the years I have been visiting the Smartbox Center, never once did I see a smartbox expert handle scrolls. Did you – ever?"

Sean hid his water gourd in the shadow of a few potato plant leaves. "No. That's what the smartboxes are all about – trying to eliminate the need to manipulate data by hand."

"Exactly, but I saw stacks and stacks of scrolls on that table. Therefore, it appears Christopher Bitsquirrel and Fred Bytesquirrel are doing something out of the ordinary. Maybe they are working on a secret project for secretary Gagwood and council squirrel Hushsquirrel? Maybe, that's why these two visited the center? Anyway – here is my plan.

"Tomorrow, we get up before dawn when everybody is still asleep. Under the protection of darkness, we climb the Smartbox Center's framework to the roof. I know there are air vents up there. I have seen the ducts on the inside of the building. From the roof we could climb into the big horizontal duct and hopefully hear what Christopher Bitsquirrel and Fred Bytesquirrel are talking about when they think they are alone. We might find out what's really going on."

"What about the guards?" Sean weighed in.

"Yep. I thought about them. I have never seen them performing any guard routines like walking around the building. They always hang out in front of the main door.

"Climbing the Smartbox Center is probably easy. That framework is practically a ladder. Once we are up there, we can figure out the rest. If it is too difficult to get back down undetected, we'll just have to wait till it's dark again. As long as we are scheduled to check the potato fields, nobody will look for us."

"Okay. Why don't we ask your Great-Grandpa what he thinks?"

"Yep, and now, let's work as slow as possible till dusk. Then we report to the Biz Center late, so they won't get suspicious tomorrow."

"Good plan," Sean agreed.

21 – STEVE LOBBYNUT AND DICK HUSHSQUIRREL

It took a bit of huffing and puffing but Great-Grandpa managed to reach his vantage point on the Big Oak. He enjoyed taking the climb every now and then. From up there he could see everything – the trees he loved so much and the valley – this was home.

But something wasn't quite right in Nuttington, and he wanted to find out what that was.

While he pondered his next move, Great-Grandpa observed the plaza in front of the burrow's main entrance. Squirrels were coming and going. Focusing on the crowd, he noticed Phillip Deerell sitting on a pine bark bench with a friend. And wasn't this Nancy Buckwheat who helped out at the library? There were so many new faces. Though Nuttington was located off the main traffic routes, it was the fastest growing and most attractive burrow in the nation. Or so it was said in the financial section of the *Nuttington Weekly Gazette.*

Whoa! Great-Grandpa squinted his eyes. Down below he saw council squirrel Dick Hushsquirrel crossing the plaza, walking and talking with Steve Lobbynut. Steve Lobbynut, that greasynut!

In Great-Grandpa's opinion Steve Lobbynut was not to be trusted. A few years ago, a reliable source had told him that Steve Lobbynut tried to get The Council to reassign funding that had been earmarked for the elementary schools' scrolls-exchange program to instead fund new seat cushions at *Nuttington Bowl.* In Great-Grandpa's opinion the idea alone was preposterous.

And council squirrel Dick Hushsquirrel? Aside from his involvement with whatever was going on at the Smartbox Center, Hushsquirrel was also pushing the idea that some of the Sciurus States' benefits, specifically – free Nuttateria food and basic education, should be cut back. Hushsquirrel also did not want the Nuttateria to be open all day, as it had always been.

And here he was, ingratiating himself to Steve Lobbynut, which seemed to suggest that Lobbynut and Hushsquirrel were working on some kind of deal.

Just thinking about Dick Hushsquirrel caused Great-Grandpa's blood pressure to rise by a few points. What had Hushsquirrel ever done that entitled him to talk about others' entitlements?

He, Great-Grandpa, could not remember ever seeing Dick Hushsquirrel working hard. For sure, he wasn't helping when during the last famine the strongest tribe members hiked for days to find a few nuts and carry them home to feed the hungry. On the flipside, Great-Grandpa had heard that, these days, Hushsquirrel and other council members accepted macadamia nut donations. Which, if true, made these acts worse – macadamia nuts were foreign imports.

Great-Grandpa was certain that the Founding Squirrels would have been outraged if they knew about this. As for Theo Roosquirrel, he even put his thoughts on record – that "This country will not be a permanently good place for any of us to live in unless we make it a reasonably good place for *all of us* to live in."

But since Theo Roosquirrel had gone on record things had changed. Today's Council often favored their own interests, especially Dick Hushsquirrel.

22 – PISTACHIO GOLD NUGGETS

Meanwhile, at the Squirrel School, classes were about to end.

Juanita thoroughly enjoyed her first day of school. The days of riding on a deer all day, not knowing where it took her and what she would find, were over. And, as if she hadn't been lucky enough to be taken in by the Roosquirrel family, at Nuttington school, she also got a chance to learn useful skills and even technology skills.

She, Juanita, was willing to do whatever it would take to stay in Nuttington and have a chance at a better life.

Eager to contribute, Juanita volunteered to sweep the classroom floor with a pine straw broom before leaving. Then she grabbed her scroll and ran to catch up with the other students. As they were passing the Smartbox Center, she was the only student who looked at the familiar building. Its door was wide open and only three guards were standing in front of it.

Arriving at the main burrow, Juanita was surprised to find Great-Grandpa waiting for her. Of course, she could not know that from his vantage point he saw the squirrel students come running up the path. "Hello Juanita, how was school?"

"Thank you, Great-Grandpa. It was fun. I can already write the words nut, bug, big, bag, bed, eat, seed, feed, tree, and squirrel. And, maybe, many more." Juanita laughed. "I took a scroll home so I could practice reading."

"Have you already made friends?"

"Not yet. I was too busy learning letters."

"Juanita, if you are interested, I can show you our library. Look – to get to the squirrel suites and the Nuttateria we'd take the left tunnel, right here at the burrow's main entrance. But to get to the library, we need to take the Boulevard Tunnel on the right. Here you'll find all kinds of neat boutiques." Great-Grandpa pointed at a row of market stands.

Juanita was stunned. Never, ever had she dreamed of a paradise like this. The closest stand presented the finest blankets woven from deer and mink hair. The next shop featured carpets made from feathers. Other boutique stands sold chestnut cups, hay mattresses, pine bark dishes, scrolls, and even woven grass bracelets and ties.

As they were passing the shops, Great-Grandpa inspected them too. Maybe, because he studied the *Smart Kuks&Quaas* the same morning, for the first time he noticed signs that said "Follow us on the *Smart Kuks&Quaas*" displayed at almost every boutique stand.

"WOW, so that's where you get all these beautiful things," exclaimed Juanita.

"Well, yes. But remember – these goods cost pistachio gold nuggets. You can earn nuggets by working a job. If you own pistachio gold, you can also start your own business."

"Where does the pistachio gold come from?"

"Pistachio gold is made from the bulbs of pistachio daffodils. The squirrel government mines them north of here, where squirrels found large deposits of these bulbs in the state of Kentucky. The Sciurus States' Pistachio Gold Depository is called Fort Knox.

"But, Great Grandpa, if the pistachio gold can be mined, why can't squirrels just simply mine it instead of working a job?"

"Clever girl!" Great-Grandpa grinned at Juanita. "You are right, this actually happened. My father used to tell of the Pistachio Gold Rush. Thousands of prospector squirrels rushed north trying to get rich quickly. Some of them did but the majority did not. Eventually, the Sciurus States' government closed off the area. Now it's a professional operation. Fort Knox is also a mint facility. There, they slice the bulbs and create the actual pistachio gold nuggets. Not much is known about the process because it occurs inside a totally secure burrow.

"And, we have arrived! See the entrance to the library, on your left, at the end of the Boulevard Tunnel?"

23 – MYSTERIES AND HINTS

As soon as Great-Grandpa and Juanita entered the library's main room, Maggie Carnegiesquir peeked through the doorway of the adjoining media room. Surprised to see Great-Grandpa, she asked, "You are back?" Then, she quickly straightened her fur.

"I hope that's okay," said Great-Grandpa, smiling. "I meant to introduce to you Miss Juanita Squirnández who has been staying with Harry and me for the last few days. Today was her first school day, and she seems to have taken a liking to reading."

"So pleased to meet you, Juanita," Maggie greeted her warmly. "I have heard much about you. Apparently, you are a fearless adventurer. I bet Harry presses you to tell him everything you experienced. Harry read every adventurer's scroll in this entire library."

"Not really," said Juanita. "He is more interested in the smartbox mystery."

"Ouch," thought Great-Grandpa, "here we go. My mistake. I should have reminded her."

"Smartbox mystery? That's not one of my scrolls," questioned Maggie Carnegiesquir.

Juanita bit her lip.

"Ahh, Maggie, I should have told you," said Great-Grandpa, in a remorseful but hushed tone. Then, he took Maggie gently by her arm and led her into the media room, away from the main entrance.

Quietly, he said, "There is really no excuse for my behavior because you and I have been friends for a long time. I can only ask that you accept my apologies for telling you little white lies. I hope you'll forgive me."

66

Maggie Carnegiesquir was stunned. Never had she seen Great-Grandpa so contrite. Did he know how she felt about him? That she thought of him as a renaissance squirrel, talented and educated, and very classy.

"Maggie, right now I cannot tell you anything about this smartbox mystery, mostly because we don't know too much. However, I am asking you – as a friend – not to mention this mystery to anybody. I really wanted to consult with you in these matters. That's why I suggested having a picnic soon. By the weekend, we… the kids and I… hope to know more. Then, I wanted to seek your input as you are one of the wisest squirrels here in Nuttington."

Maggie Carnegiesquir smiled and said, "That's quite alright. Like I said – your secrets are safe with me. Allow me to offer one tidbit that might help – this morning Bill Gatsquirrel left on an extended business trip."

Now it was Great-Grandpa's turn to be surprised. Obviously, Maggie knew more than she let on. But it was too dangerous to ask more questions. Cee-Kee could be close-by.

"Thank you, Maggie. You don't know how much I appreciate your friendship and support. I'll be in touch regarding the picnic. Adieu." Great-Grandpa bowed, gently took Maggie Carnegiesquir's paw, and touched it with his lips. As he was about to turn and leave, two squirrels dashed through the door.

"We made it," Harry burst out and then bowed to Maggie. "Good evening, Mrs. Carnegiesquir. How do you do? Sean and I came to pick up Great-Grandpa."

"Hello you two. How nice to see you. I hope to see more of you this weekend. And now, if you'll excuse me, I have to close up the library."

While Maggie Carnegiesquir covered the smartboxes with clear plastic sheets, she pondered what she had learned. Apparently, Great-Grandpa and Harry too thought that something was rotten in the Sciurus States. As a dedicated librarian and an ever-curious researcher, Maggie didn't like to guess. Still, the two facts she knew suggested that something odd was happening.

Most certainly, it seemed like a strange coincidence that she had been asked to limit the library visitors' use of the smartboxes while Bill Gatsquirrel left for an extended business trip. Maggie Carnegiesquir could not wait to hear what Great-Grandpa and the kids found out.

24 – A SECOND PICNIC

As they had done the day before, Harry and Sean went to pick up dinner while Great-Grandpa, and Juanita walked ahead to their picnic place. Juanita wondered if Great-Grandpa was mad at her for revealing their secret. She hoped and guessed that Maggie Carnegiesquir wasn't going to tell anybody. Because Maggie liked Great-Grandpa. Which was obvious. And he liked her too.

Meanwhile, Great-Grandpa was wondering about the weather. Normally, a cool wind blew over the ridge but today, again, there wasn't even the tiniest breeze. By now, the Dog Days of Summer seemed to last forever. The air was hot and sticky, every day. He mused that this was probably how this type of weather got its name. In the past, dogs used to hunt squirrels. Dogs who were in hot pursuit of squirrels stuck their sticky noses into everything. They had been known to breathe into squirrels' burrows. Or so he had heard.

Once Harry and Sean arrived with the food, everybody started eating but Harry did not. Instead, he laid out his idea about climbing the Smartbox Center and spying on Christopher Bitsquirrel and Fred Bytesquirrel. "What do you think, Great-Grandpa?" he asked.

"Well, it might be a great idea. Let me quickly share what I found out today. It might be useful information that helps you in making a decision."

Sean stopped chewing on his acorn, Juanita got nervous again, and Harry just smiled confidently. In his mind, Great-Grandpa was the gray eminence of Nuttington who possessed an unrivaled talent to snoop out information and connect any and all dots.

"Kids – everything I share is confidential. This is third party information, albeit from a very trustworthy source." For a second, Great-Grandpa fixed his eyes on Juanita.

Then, he continued. "I visited the library today. Maggie Carnegiesquir told me that – A – she and Mr. Khansquirrel have been instructed to limit the library visitors' and the students' usage of the smartboxes and – B – Bill Gatsquirrel left on an extended business trip."

Great-Grandpa cleared his throat. "I am not terribly talented when it comes to smartbox related affairs but what happened in the last few days is so odd, that even I noticed it.

"For years, the Smartbox Center's door was open every day and nobody ever tried to limit the usage of the smartboxes. In fact, it seemed to me, Nuttington's influencers pushed the tribe to use the smartboxes more and more. What could have happened that they felt a need to go on lock-down?

"Also, it seems kind of strange that Bill Gatsquirrel left on an extended business trip at a time when Christopher and Fred are performing some kind of major maintenance operation. Wouldn't he want to be here when important affairs are happening?"

Sean spoke first. "That's what I think. Throughout the years I went to school, Bill Gatsquirrel was working at the Brainhub, almost every day."

Harry had other thoughts. "I am more surprised by the fact that secretary Chip Gagwood and council squirrel Dick Hushsquirrel visited the Smartbox Center. Nuttington's officials hardly ever visit the Center. They prefer to have somebody bring them the reports. I know because I worked at the Brainhub during my sophomore year."

Finally, Juanita asked, "And what about Cee-Kee watching Great-Grandpa?"

For a second, all of them sat in silence. Certainly, the fact that Cee-Kee was watching Great-Grandpa made the least sense. Great-Grandpa himself admitted that he had little interest in using smartboxes.

Great-Grandpa broke the silence. "There is something else. Today I checked the *Smart Kuks&Quaas.*" He grinned. "All by myself. To my surprise I found kuks & quaas about #ecommerce, #cryptonuts, and #nuthacking. What's that? Especially the #nuthacking."

Harry nodded. "That's a totally new thing for entrepreneur squirrels. How to make lots of pistachio gold. I don't really know how it works but I heard the Biz Center is going to offer training courses in the near future."

"I don't understand," Great-Grandpa replied. "On one paw, the use of smartboxes is supposed to be limited. On the other hand, new programs for entrepreneur squirrels are being offered. Can you kids explain how these two fit together?"

Frustrated, Harry jumped up and walked in circles around the group. "We don't know. Nothing makes sense. That's just it. So, what do you think about Sean and me spying on Christopher Bitsquirrel and Fred Bytesquirrel?"

"It's probably a great idea. Follow the pistachios... and the macadamia nuts. But listen, Harry – tomorrow is Friday. This morning, Gary Logisquir reminded me that tomorrow is a party night – 'Friday Lake Night.' Most Nuttingtonians will attend. Probably, the majority of the party goers will sleep in the next day. Which reduces the chance that you boys get caught. Waiting one day won't do any harm."

For a moment, Harry seemed taken aback but a minute later he grinned. "Right on, Great-Grandpa. That's an excellent plan."

Sean seemed even more relieved.

25 – "FRIDAY LAKE NIGHT"

As expected, Harry suffered through Friday. Sean and he spent all day working the second potato field. In the meantime, Juanita attended classes and Great-Grandpa attempted to spy on Steve Lobbynut and council squirrel Dick Hushsquirrel. An hour before lunch time, he took up position on one of the pine bark benches in front of the burrow's main entrance and pretended to read a scroll. If either Steve Lobbynut or Dick Hushsquirrel passed by on their way to the Nuttateria, he'd be able to see them. No such luck though. Neither one of them came by.

Later in the day, Great-Grandpa visited the government center to find out when the next burrow hall meeting was scheduled to take place. Most certainly, he would attend this event, the coming Wednesday. Then he visited the library to invite Maggie Carnegiesquir to their family picnic on Sunday afternoon. He told her he'd send Harry to pick her up.

Finally, the sun started setting and the squirrels got ready for "Friday Lake Night." Juanita carefully brushed her coat with a holly leaf. The day before, Harry helped her to break off the tips of its thorns, thereby turning the holly leaf into a neat brush. She noticed that her fur looked much shinier. Then, Sean arrived. He had gone home after work to tell his parents that he was going to sleep over at Harry's after the party.

By the time Great-Grandpa and the kids arrived at the lake, the summer party was in full swing. The atmosphere was beautiful. The stage and all picnic tables around the lake were lit by firefly lamps. Squirrels were splashing in the water; others were playing tag in the trees. Again others crowded around the stage to listen to Nuttington's most famous balladeer Johnny Cashsquirrel. Presently, Johnny Cashsquirrel sang his signature song, "Everybody Loves a Nut."

Johnny Cashsquirrel's real name was Howie Nuttie. He grew up in Nushville, an outpost in the Southwest Territory. Howie, a.k.a. Johnny Cashsquirrel, swore that, in Nushville, his ancestors had lived in the yard of a human who used to sing "Everybody Loves a Nut."

Since Howie never learned the original lyrics, he made up new ones. And he swore his lyrics were much easier to remember, which was obvious when looking at the enthused audience who sang along with the chorus.

> The nuts on the trees are falling down ♫
> falling down, falling down ♫
> The nuts on the trees are falling down ♫
> All through the towne. ♫

Howie also came up with verses about finding trees that carry chestnuts, climbing trees to gather pine nuts, filling baskets with acorns, and cracking shells to get to the hazelnuts.

A few years ago, his song was made the national anthem by unanimous resolution from The Council.

After receiving this honor, Howie had taken the stage name Johnny Cashsquirrel to honor his idol. He also liked to pay tribute to this human every time he sang the song. And, though many squirrels were glad that the humans who drove around in rolling boxes were gone, Howie frequently mentioned that humans were not inherently dangerous. Obviously, any species that brought forth an artist who crooned about nuts had to be of good nature.

Howie Nuttie also knew other stories about the humans. He'd tell of little humans who in the fall hurled stones at chestnut trees so they could collect the nuts that fell down. According to Howie, the little humans built puppets from the nuts. "They used the chestnuts for toys." Another likable trait.

Suddenly, without warning, the applause for Johnny Cashsquirrel was interrupted by a dangerous sounding "Ping – pong – pong – pong." Juanita froze. "Humans' BB guns?" she wondered. She had heard about these dangerous weapons.

However, the party guests did not try to seek shelter. After a momentary pause, they laughed and clapped even harder. Harry and Sean

high-fived each other and joined the crowd in chanting, "POP …
CORN… POP … CORN … POP … CORN."

"Come on, Juanita, let's line up. They are serving popcorn," Harry
shouted, grabbed her by the paw, and with Sean ran towards a booth
close to the lake shore at the north end. While they lined up with dozens
of other excited-looking squirrels, Juanita asked, "What is pop-corn?"

Harry grinned. "Good stuff. It's heated, puffed corn kernels."

"Heated? As in fire?" Juanita looked shocked.

"Yep. You probably can't see his machine from here, but do you see
that squirrel gentleman with the grayish white fur over there? The one
with a grass bow tie?

"That's Thomas Edinut, one of our greatest inventors. He con-
structed a machine that uses a humans' mirror to create fire. The culinary
arts squirrels use the fire to heat a light metal pan. They pour peanut oil
and dried corn kernels into the pan and shake it. When you hear the corn
popping, just like now, the popcorn is done. Unfortunately, it's a difficult
and dangerous process. That's why they don't make popcorn very often.
Probably, they did today because Johnny Cashsquirrel is performing."

26 – CEE-KEE ALLSQUIRREL

While most squirrels raced to line up at the popcorn stand, Great-Grandpa decided to secure a log table. Before he could even sit down, someone patted him on the back. It was Gary Logisquir.

"Gary, you party animal, why aren't you getting popcorn?"

"I am looking for victims. As always." Gary Logisquir cackled. "Want to play nut-checkers?"

Great-Grandpa laughed heartily. Then he said, "Sure," before scanning the crowd a last time. He was not surprised to notice Cee-Kee Allsquirrel who seemed to examine the line of squirrels waiting next to the popcorn stand. "There she is again," he mumbled.

"Who?" Gary wanted to know.

"Cee-Kee Allsquirrel. I don't know what it is with this girl but, lately, she seems to follow me around." Great-Grandpa chuckled with a puzzled undertone.

"Cee-Kee? I am betting three pistachios she isn't following *you*," replied Gary Logisquir, matter-of-factly.

"Gary, I love your dry humor, but I swear, she is following me. It was actually Harry who noticed it first."

"Holy peanut, she isn't following you. I am betting three pistachios she is following Juanita."

"Juanita? What makes you say that?" Great-Grandpa sounded genuinely surprised.

Gary looked around, then bent his head toward Great-Grandpa and said in a confidential tone, "This is between us. Last year, I attended the National Nut-Checkers Championship in Virginia. And who do I meet, totally by chance? – Cee-Kee Allsquirrel. But Cee-Kee Allsquirrel does not play nut-checkers. You know what else is in Virginia? The headquarters of our Central Kernel Agency."

Great-Grandpa's mouth dropped open. "Are you trying to say…"

Gary shook his head and cut him off. "I am not trying to say anything. But I have heard that the Central Kernel Agency is watching dark-furred foreigners. Also, you must admit – Juanita's story is pretty crazy."

He continued in an exaggerated but hushed voice, "Young squirrel girl crosses half the continent alone by herself without getting killed… It sounds like a fairy tale… You can't really be surprised if Cee-Kee is watching her, you, and the boys. Of course, that is, if, indeed, Cee-Kee is working for the Central Kernel Agency. Which I don't know for sure."

Great-Grandpa was stunned. Of course, everything Gary said made sense. But, why, and how, had things come to this? Since its early days the squirrel republic had always welcomed immigrants of all colors. In fact, neither this nor any other large burrow could have been built without the contributions of thousands of immigrant squirrels. Even Howie Nuttie, a.k.a. Johnnie Cashsquirrel, was an immigrant.

Irked, Great-Grandpa lost the game in only seventeen moves.

As he sorted the game pieces, he returned to the subject. "Y'know, Gary, I am irritated by what you told me. Though I see the logic in your thoughts, I wonder if this is what the Founding Squirrels aimed for. The way I see it, our squirrels' way of living seems to be changing – slowly, but steadily."

"Spot on," Gary came back. "Lately, I see a lot of change. Also, at least to me, it seems there is no plan."

"When you play nut-checkers, you have to have a plan at all times. And – you need to adjust it, depending on how the game goes. But our council doesn't seem to do that. When they discover a problem – I heard that, apparently, the potato harvest was a bust – their only plan is to cut our benefits. Never theirs.

"Two weeks ago, when I attended the last burrow hall meeting, I heard that presumptuous Dick Hushsquirrel talk about cutting benefits. When I heard this, I thought things were dire, but today, the tribe is celebrating as if we had a record harvest. Does that make sense? Not to me."

"I think that's part of their plan." Great-Grandpa drawled. "Squirrels who get to party feel good. And squirrels who feel good don't ask questions. Also, the Council cancelled quite a few burrow hall meetings in the recent past. I myself plan to attend the next one, next Wednesday. That is – if it takes place."

Right then, Harry, Sean and Juanita returned with a big basket of popcorn.

After removing his game to make room for the food, Gary said to Great-Grandpa, "I am very pleased that you'll attend the meeting. The tribe listens to you. Somebody needs to remind them of what our republic is all about.

"That this nation's founding fathers declared that, to have a perfect union, we need promote the general welfare of *all* citizens.

"Which only makes sense. Because, if the general welfare of all citizens was not the goal, all of us might as well strike out on our own and live isolated on our own trees."

"That's what happened to us," said Juanita. "That's how we lived on the barrier island. And that's why nobody could help us when that terrible storm struck."

Gary Logisquir peered at her. "What a clever girl! She explained it better than I did. Juanita, maybe you should run for office?"

Before Gary Logisquir could expound on that idea, Harry quickly said, "Sean and I are going to look around a bit, check out who of our friends is at the party. We'll see you later." As soon as they were out of Gary's sight, the boys took a detour and returned to the burrow. They wanted to take a long nap before embarking on their spy mission.

27 – HARRY'S SPY MISSION

Not surprisingly, Harry had no trouble waking up in the middle of the night. He was ready. In his mind he had rehearsed what he'd do more than a hundred times.

He quickly downed a cup of water, awakened Sean, offered him water, grabbed his own bag with provisions, and gave Sean his bag. A minute later, they were on their way.

As they moved silently through the tunnel system, the teens were surprised to hear unexpected noises. Many squirrels were snoring, some rather loudly, in their apartments. Harry grinned. As always, Great-Grandpa had been right. It sounded like most of the party-goers would sleep in this Saturday morning.

Feeling a lot less nervous, the two friends strode down into the valley. Sean thought they couldn't have picked a better night. Not one owl, fox, or coyote was out looking for prey, in the pale light of the moon.

Finally, the boys got close enough to the Smartbox Center to observe the building and its guards.

A single firefly lamp lit the entrance of the building. Two guards sat on the threshold playing mouse bone dice and the third guard leaned against the closed door, either dozing or sleeping.

The conditions seemed so perfect that Harry felt irritated. Over and over, he scanned the surrounding woods, the skies, and the area between the façade rod system and the building. But – nothing. No additional guards, no predators, not even a harmless bat. So, he gave the "good to go"-sign and Sean and he climbed up to the roof.

There, Sean took over as the mission's technical specialist. Expertly, he crawled underneath the metal dome that covered the main air vent to see if it was protected by wire mesh netting designed to keep squirrels and birds out of the ducts. It was.

But, as luck had it, all the screws which held the netting in place appeared to be rusty. Sean knew why that was. No human had been here in a long time.

He sank his nails under the netting next to one of the screws and pulled gently on the mesh. The screw snapped easily, like an acorn stem. Once Sean had removed the entire netting, Harry joined him. Together, they looked down at the vertical ventilation pipe.

"Perfect," whispered Sean. "This duct has snap lock seams. See the ridges? That's where the individual pieces snap together. We'll use 'em like a ladder. After you."

Slowly, Harry descended into the vent pipe. Pretty soon, he could see the large, horizontal duct he'd been looking for. It was close. Harry jumped. He felt something like soft cushioning under his feet. Then, a huge cloud of dust spread.

OMSG! What's this stuff?

"Ah-choo. Ahchoo. Ah-choo."

After the dust cleared a bit, Harry looked down the duct, on both sides. On his right, he could see a huge fan at the end of the air vent. The moon shone through its openings and illuminated the duct.

"Pretty neat," Harry thought. Though the fan was not moving, fresh air could enter the duct through this hole. Plus, it was a potential escape route.

Unfortunately, things looked rather disastrous on the other side. The bottom of the vent pipe was covered with dust as far as Harry could see; in fact, the layers of dust appeared to be higher, the farther away from the opening with the fan. Who knew how high the coat of dust was, sixty squirrel jumps inside the building?

Harry remembered what one of his instructors at the academy used to preach all the time – "Always remember – Noise attracts predators. Noise means detection."

Of course, presently there was no danger. Christopher and Fred weren't due to arrive until the sun came up. Still, Sean and he might be in trouble later in the day. Would they be able to suppress sneezing and coughing for an entire day?

Harry felt a panic attack coming on.

Then he thought of Juanita and how she rode on a wooden board during a huge storm. And of Great-Grandpa when he said, "Maybe you boys should venture out of Nuttington every now and then and learn to deal with new challenges?"

If Juanita could surf on a wooden board, Sean and he could manage this problem. At least, he hoped so.

Harry moved away from the vertical pipe and hissed, "Good to go."

"Ahchoo. Ahchoo." Sean landed next to him. Harry smiled and whispered, "Hey, engineering whiz, check out this dust. My best plan is to try walking like storks, very slowly. I hope you have something better."

Sean examined the dusty duct. "We have water gourds and I have one large woven grass towel in my bag. I'll fix us up once we are in position."

Walking through the dusty duct seemed to take forever. By the time Harry and Sean arrived at the part of the duct they believed to be right above the smartbox, they were exhausted.

"Don't sit down yet," Sean warned and pulled the grass towel out of his bag. Methodically, he bit through the towel, splitting it into two parts. Then he carefully poured water over one piece and handed it to Harry. "Hold this over your mouth while you sit down."

Waiting in the duct proved to be a test of willpower. Dust was everywhere. They sat in dust, they were covered in dust, dust had crept into their noses and coated their throats. Both boys would have liked to brush the dust at least off their faces but knew better. Even the tiniest movement would stir up more dust. So, the boys prepared themselves for a long and unpleasant wait.

28 – SCREECHES

After what seemed like an eternity, the sound of a creaking door awakened the dozing teens. Shuffling footsteps could be heard. Screech... screech... Somebody was moving something down below.

"At least today we can work uninterrupted."

"I am telling you we are doing all this work for nothing."

"Weasel dung. Bill will save the day."

Screech... screech...

"... irresponsible..."

Screech... screech...

"... I am telling you it's not sustainable."

"So far, we found five hundred twenty-four good..."

Screech... screech...

"... that's only about twenty-five percent."

Sitting as still as possible in the duct, Harry regretted that he could not take notes but not holding the wet towel over his mouth was not an option.

"Another sixty-eight bags to go..."

Screech ... screech...

Annoyed, Harry squeezed his knuckles to avoid bursting out in anger. He was trembling from tiredness and frustration. Here they were, so close, and he still could not understand the whole conversation. Shortly thereafter even the screeching subsided, and the downstairs fell quiet. Eventually, Sean whispered through his towel, "What now?"

"They are probably working," hissed Harry. "We can't move. It's too dangerous."

After a while, both boys dozed off again.

29 – NEW INFORMATION

"Christopher, come on. It's lunch time. If you wait any longer, we won't get a table in the Nuttateria."

The loud shout startled Harry and Sean. They heard somebody moving below, then it became quiet again.

Once he was sure that Christopher and Fred had left, Harry whispered, "I think we are done here. It seems Christopher and Fred aren't working in the same room so we probably won't hear anything once they are back. Let's move out before we forget the few things we did hear or, worse – get found out."

The thought of fresh air sped up the boys' movements. Back on the roof, they brushed off the dust as best as they could. Then, they made themselves comfortable in the shade of one of the blue panels. Looking around, Harry noticed a funny looking small, blue panel in a corner. It was mounted on an even funnier looking box.

But Harry didn't check it out. He felt it was more important to write down everything he overheard while his memory was still fresh. He pulled a quill and a scroll out of his bag. In his best handwriting, he made a bulleted list.

- THINKS THEY ARE DOING ALL OF THE WORK FOR NOTHING
- BILL (GATSQUIRREL???) WILL SAVE THE DAY
- IRRESPONSIBLE AND NOT SUSTAINABLE
- FOUND 524 (?) GOOD
- = ONLY 25%
- 68 BAGS TO GO

Next, he drew a sketch of the two ducts they crawled through, complete with annotations of distances and the dimensions of the pipe.

Studying the information he said, "We don't know much, but we know there is a problem. Clearly, it is something related to smartboxes, because Christopher and Fred are in fact working on it. But the problem can't be a smartbox problem because we don't even have 524 smartboxes in all Nuttington. So, it's got to be a power kernel problem.

"Also, one of them thinks that Bill will save the day. Remember that Mrs. Carnegiesquir said that Bill Gatsquirrel left on an extended business trip? I bet he is trying to get power kernels. But what's with the 68 bags? And why does one of them think that they are doing all the work for nothing?"

Sean sighed. "I can't think right now. I am itching all over. My brain feels paralyzed. Do you think we can leave?"

Harry shook his head. "Too risky. The best way to wash off all that dust is to take a dip in the lake. But by now even the squirrels who drank pecan liquor will be up.

"It's Saturday afternoon and it is hot. Probably, half of Nuttington will be at the beach. If they see us, full of dust, tuft to toe, somebody is going to ask questions. We've got to stay here until the sun sets."

30 – THE MAP

Meanwhile, mid-Saturday morning, Maggie Carnegiesquir went to open the library. She was pleased to see that Nuttington burrow was quiet – not one visitor was waiting in front of the library door. The scrolls needed to be sorted and the library shelves needed to be dusted. This type of work could be done much faster if she wasn't interrupted all the time.

The tedious work kept Maggie busy till lunch time. Later, she dusted the rooms and swept all floors. Once done with that, she calculated the visitors' numbers. Finally, she examined her records to see how many scrolls were overdue or lost.

When by late afternoon still no visitors showed up, Maggie Carnegiesquir decided to check the two smartboxes' data usage. Maybe Christopher Bitsquirrel or Bill Gatsquirrel were interested in this information.

On one of the two smartboxes seven megabytes had been used, but on the other one more than thirty-six. How was this possible? Maggie Carnegiesquir was certain she had asked every visitor to limit their usage of the smartboxes.

She took a sip of chilled dandelion water from her gourd. Slowly, a memory began to form in her mind. On Thursday morning, council squirrel Frank Indienut had visited with his wife. He said he wanted to check the *Smart Kuks&Quaas* while she selected story scrolls for the kids. Laura Indienut had been particularly annoying on that day, wanting to see more and more scrolls. Maggie Carnegiesquir could not remember how long Frank Indienut had been alone in the media room.

Since Laura Indienut had bogged her down with a thousand questions, Maggie did not even ask her husband how long he wanted to use one of the smartboxes.

Frank Indienut was a regular, his wife was not. He visited the library to check his *Smart Kuks&Quaas* account about once every full moon.

But even if he had posted dozens of kuk-quaas he could not have used that many megabytes.

Had Frank Indienut checked out goods on the trading platform? Maggie needed to know. She'd prefer it if he stayed away from that site until Christopher Bitsquirrel and Fred Bytesquirrel were done with whatever they were doing. Ever curious, she tapped the menu button on the top of the browser window and then the "history"-button.

Perplexed, she noticed that somebody had looked at a site with the URL Weather.Universal.Net. Maggie Carnegiesquir had never heard of this site so she accessed it.

It showed a map of the continent albeit with much more nuance than she had ever seen. Whereas the squirrels' scroll maps had mainly white spaces west of the Sciurus States, this one was all filled in. Even more shockingly – the map showed a huge red blob southwest of the Sciurus States. It was getting bigger before Maggie's eyes. In horror, she watched how the red blob expanded and then collapsed. And again it expanded and collapsed. And again. At its biggest, the huge red blob covered almost the entire bottom of the map.

Who was Weather.Universal.Net? And why did Frank Indienut know about this site even though she, Maggie, did not?

There was no text, no words that described the map. Then again, Maggie Carnegiesquir knew instinctively that this weather map showed an insanely hot heat storm creeping north-northeast. Naturally, she could not tell how far away these places were but somewhere southwest of Nuttington a disaster was unfolding.

Maggie Carnegiesquir was aghast. *What should she do? What could she do?*

She turned off the smartbox and hung a sign "Will Be Right Back" next to the library door. Then she walked to the lake, hastily.

Maggie needed fresh air and – the sight of water.

It being late afternoon, only a few squirrels were at the lake. Maggie Carnegiesquir sat down at the picnic table that was farthest from the beach.

Having removed herself from the hypnotizing picture, she thought through what she discovered. *Who else knew about this site?* Somehow, Maggie Carnegiesquir found it hard to believe that council squirrel Frank Indienut was the only squirrel who knew about this site.

Indienut was a quiet red squirrel whose main agendas were higher education and advanced manufacturing. He liked to talk about the need for safety laws and basic labor laws. Frank Indienut always did things the proper way. If Indienut were to know about an impending catastrophe, for sure, he'd tell others. Which implied, The Council knew about this site.

The sun started to go down and the squirrel parents collected their pups. The last beachgoers left. But Maggie stayed where she was. She felt paralyzed. She could think of only one thing – the huge, red blob.

Suddenly, the noise of running footsteps interrupted the eerie silence. To Maggie's surprise, they did not come from the burrow's back entrance but from a path that led around the burrow to the Brainhub. Mr. Khansquirrel was known to take that path when he took his students swimming. Two squirrels emerged from the darkness and jumped into the lake. One of them called out, "Whoohoo, this feels sooo good."

Maggie Carnegiesquir froze at the sound of the voice. It sounded like Harry's. She squinted her eyes. No doubt about it – the two squirrels splashing in the lake were Harry and Sean. As fast as they came, they ran off.

"What was that about?" Maggie thought. Why were the boys out late, alone by themselves?

She remembered that both boys had taken the Expedition-Exploration course. Maybe, in that course, they also learned about weather systems and weather maps? Tomorrow, she'd get a chance to ask them.

31 – THE 'SQUARE DEAL FOR SQUIRRELS'

On Sunday morning, Great-Grandpa took Juanita out for breakfast to the Nuttateria. The special of the day was "One tiny bird egg, sprinkled with bugleweed seeds and a side order of chopped pecans."

As the attendant handed Juanita two plates with pretty food arrangements, she could only wonder, "Why did we never come up with this idea?" On the island they had eaten all foods separately.

But Juanita knew why that was. On the island, her family and friends had struggled to survive, every day. In contrast, Nuttington's residents had time to think about how they wanted to present their foods.

Soon thereafter, Gary Logisquir arrived. And after a few minutes of chit-chat, he asked the question Great-Grandpa dreaded, "Say, where are the boys??"

Juanita immediately lowered her head and began rearranging the chopped pecans on her plate. An awkward pause ensued. Finally, Great-Grandpa replied casually, "Harry and Sean? They are probably out and about."

"Boiled peanuts," Gary Logisquir snorted. "I can sense that you guys are hiding something."

Great-Grandpa looked up from his plate. "Are we done here? Let's go outside and visit the pine grove. It's such a pretty morning." Without asking why Great-Grandpa did not want to talk inside the Nuttateria, Gary got up.

And so it came about that Great-Grandpa told his friend about the closed door, the guards, secretary Chip Gagwood and council squirrel Dick Hushsquirrel visiting the center, and that Harry and Sean were investigating these strange occurrences.

"Clever boys. Great move!" commented Gary Logisquir with a deeply satisfied voice. "The nutty truth is we don't know anything. The Council gives us fewer and fewer specific answers. We are nut tokens in their game."

Juanita chimed in. "I thought The Council governs the Sciurus States."

"Indeed," Gary Logisquir grunted. "You are right. Which is precisely why special interest groups are trying to influence them. It's called lobbying. Lobbying is a process in which individual Bignut squirrels or squirrel groups try to sway The Council's decisions in their favor.

"When Theo Roosquirrel became president, similar activities were going on. But Roosquirrel thought that it's the president's job to do what's best for all squirrels, rich and poor. And when he saw that some squirrel industrialists yielded too much power, he broke apart their trusts.

"Now, only a few generations later, some council squirrels favor again the interests of groups who can afford to send lobbyist squirrels… Lobbyist squirrels who bear gifts. Mostly macadamia nuts."

Juanita's mouth dropped open.

"There are all kinds of problems," Great-Grandpa agreed. "The deer told me that in part of the country the infrastructure is crumbling. Also, foreign field workers are not appreciated the way they used to be."

Gary grimaced. "And my sources tell me there are plans to outsource manufacturing to other countries, outside the Sciurus States. The Council likes a new kind of business called ecommerce. They believe that's the future of business."

"Oh, you know about that?" Great-Grandpa interrupted. "Did you check the *Smart Kuks&Quaas*? There are dozens of kuks-quaas about #ecommerce, #cryptonuts, and #nuthacking. I saw them the other day."

"FOXEYE! That's it," grumbled Gary Logisquir. "And somebody is going to make a lot of pistachio gold from these deals. I believe The Council is forgetting what squirrelity really means. My sources tell me that the Sciurus States' smaller burrows which don't have smartboxes will depend on nut donations, sooner or later. If they don't depend on them already."

Great-Grandpa sighed. "If Theo Roosquirrel saw what some of our council squirrels are doing, he'd have them by their tails."

"Darn right you are," Gary nodded. "Didn't Theo Roosquirrel say, 'The most practical kind of politics is the politics of decency'?"

"Yep, he did," Great-Grandpa agreed. "That's why he came up with the 'Square Deal for Squirrels.'"

"These days everything is unsquare," Gary Logisquir acknowledged. "It's the same with what the kids' friends are doing. I believe the *YoungNutcrackers* are right. The academy is unsquare too. Sure, it's a fine school, probably the finest academy in the nation. But their prices? My nephew's son who lives in Salemnutterry visited the academy to check it out. He says they want to be paid in macadamia nuts. That's rather scandalous."

He looked at Juanita. "You know what you should do? You kids should expand your grassroots movement to other burrows. Get bigger, get stronger."

"What a great idea. Thank you." Juanita smiled enthusiastically.

"Gary, I am sorry, but we have got to," announced Great-Grandpa. "I invited Maggie Carnegiesquir to a picnic this afternoon. I still have a few things to do, like picking up provisions, right now."

"That's quite alright. I must practice my game. The National Nut-Checkers Championship in Shenandoah is coming up. I intend to win it."

32 – CONNECTING THE DOTS

Later that afternoon, Harry went to the library to pick up Maggie Carnegiesquir. As he entered, he saw her standing in the media room, looking at one of the smartboxes.

"Hello, Harry," she greeted him. "Could you come over here and look at this smartbox site and tell me what you think this is?"

The second Harry looked at the map with its expanding red blob, he felt a scare like nothing he had experienced before.

"Mrs. Carnegiesquir, how 'd you get this?" he whispered nervously.

"I'll tell you later. What do you think it is?"

"This map is human made, that's for sure," Harry said. "No squirrel I know could create that. So, there really are humans alive, somewhere. This is a heat storm, isn't it?"

"I believe so. Let me close this out before we go and see your Great-Grandpa."

Not surprisingly the picnic turned into a different kind of picnic. While Great-Grandpa, Juanita, Harry, and Sean nervously nibbled on a few nuts, Maggie Carnegiesquir told them about the map with the scary red blob and how she uncovered council squirrel Frank Indienut's secret. She ended her story by saying, "I believe Frank Indienut has known about this site for a long time, probably – for more than a year. Because that's how long he's been visiting the library, at least once every full moon.

"But his behavior is atypical. The squirrels who are really into the *Smart Kuks&Quaas* typically read them every day, or every other day. Maybe Frank Indienut never looked at the *Smart Kuks&Quaas* but instead kept tabs on this site? Unfortunately, I don't know. Though I always ask all visitors what they plan to do, I never look over their shoulders."

Great-Grandpa nodded, thoughtfully. "Maggie, if I may suggest… Can we invite Gary Logisquir? He's been one of my very good friends for a long time. And he is very smart."

As soon as she said yes, Great-Grandpa sent out the boys to look for Gary. And when all three returned Maggie got to tell her story again.

In his typical style, Gary Logisquir honed in on the issue immediately. "Maggie, I'd love to see this site but first: Do you have any idea how Frank Indienut could have learned about the site?"

When Maggie shook her head, Gary continued, "And, Maggie, you say this blob is happening in the Southwest? Wouldn't this be where Juanita came from? Could the storm that killed Juanita's tribe have something to do with this?"

"Holy pistachio! You are right. I was so in shock, I didn't even think about that. Most certainly these weather events could be related."

Maggie Carnegiesquir turned to Juanita. "Juanita, dear, how long did it take you to get here?"

Juanita seemed shaken. Finally, she said, "Ten full moons, maybe eleven. I can't remember. These were very difficult days. Especially before I met the deer who work for the Deer Express."

"Thank you, Juanita, don't worry, that guess is good enough," Maggie patted her on the shoulder. Then, she turned to Gary. "It seems the region where the storm hovers is far away. Still, the weather is warmer than last year. No doubt about it."

Meanwhile, Harry sat in silence. Sean and he had planned to tell what they had found out, at the picnic. They thought they discovered a big secret. As it turned out, Maggie Carnegiesquir had discovered an even bigger secret. *How many mysteries were there, happening simultaneously?* Finally, he wondered out loud, "So, how does all of this fit to the power kernel problem?"

Surprised, Maggie turned to him and asked, "Harry, what are you talking about?"

Harry presented his list and told Maggie, Great-Grandpa, and Gary Logisquir what Sean and he learned on their spy mission.

93

"Ultra-rancid peanut stew!"

Gary Logisquir jumped up, walked a tiny circle, and sat down again. "This story is getting wilder and wilder by the minute. What I don't understand is, how could seventy-five percent of the power kernels could have gone bad?"

"They could be rusty," suggested Sean. "On our spy mission we encountered rust."

"Okay, that's an excellent thought. Which leads to the next question – Are these two events connected? The thing our smartbox technicians are working on and Frank Indienut's weather site?"

"I don't know how they might be connected," declared Great-Grandpa, "but my sixth sense tells me that they are. Nuttington has been moving on the same steady track since Steve I'Squirrel introduced his smartbox. Now, all of a sudden, all of these unusual things happen – all at once? I don't believe in coincidences. So – what do you think we should do?"

"Citizenship in a Republic ..." Maggie Carnegiesquir suggested, thoughtfully. "The squirrel who really counts in the world is the doer..."

Great-Grandpa gazed at her in total admiration. "You can quote Theo Roosqirrel's speeches? And thank you for reminding me of this important speech."

Maggie smiled and quoted some more, "It is the doer of deeds who actually counts in the battle for life." Great-Grandpa nodded thoughtfully. Noticing that the youngsters stared at him and Maggie, he cleared his throat and said, "Kids, Mrs. Carnegiesquir quoted from one of Theo Roosquirrel's most important speeches, 'Citizenship in a Republic.'

"I think Mrs. Carnegiesquir wanted to remind me, in a gentle way, that I need to be a doer of deeds, like Theo's speech outlined. Maybe, lately I decided to 'wait and see' a few times too often.

"And now, Maggie, why don't you take us to the library and show us this site."

33 – THE BLOB

Actually seeing the huge, red blob with their own eyes, as it expanded and contracted, again and again, came as a shock for Juanita, Sean, Great-Grandpa, and Gary Logisquir. Indeed, Great-Grandpa was so horrified that his legs felt shaky, and he had to sit down.

Maggie Carnegiesquir who watched the blob for the third time could not help but wonder how Frank Indienut managed to keep his secret, for such a long time. When she first saw the blob she wanted to scream, and nothing had changed about that.

But she did not allow herself to get emotional. As calmly as possible she said, "There is Texas, northwest of the water," and pointed at the map. "The little, long specs are the barrier islands. Nuttington is over here, on the eastern side of the land, where you see the big mountains. When the blob fully expands it comes closer, but it never reaches the west side of the mountains. Also, the part of the blob that comes closest to us isn't red, but orange."

Sean raised his arm. "Mrs. Carnegiesquir, I just have a question," he said shyly. "Is it possible that the heat storm destroyed Juanita's island, then went away, and now it came back? I mean, is it possible that the storm comes and goes?"

"Hm," replied Maggie Carnegiesquir. "Somehow, I don't believe that. I think when Frank Indienut visited the library last Thursday, he brought his wife along for the sole purpose of distracting me. This implies he already knew what he was going to see!"

From the tone of her voice, Gary Logisquir could sense that Maggie was still upset with Frank Indienut's efforts to trick her. Gently, he put his paw on Maggie's arm. "Maggie, allow me... as this is a problem of logical deduction.

"You are one hundred percent correct. It is a given that Frank Indienut knew what he was going to see. Because he did something he'd never done before – he tried to make sure that you would not see what he was doing. If he wanted to check out Goldfinch feather rugs made in Maryland, he didn't need to go through that trouble.

"But – doesn't the fact that Frank Indienut involved his wife also suggest that he knew that you had been asked to limit the usage of the smartboxes? At least to me, it seems that's the only logical conclusion."

Maggie Carnegiesquir and Great-Grandpa nodded in silent agreement, and the kids gaped at Gary, completely baffled.

After a short pause, Gary continued. "So – apparently – somebody informed Frank Indienut that Maggie might be looking over his shoulder.

"If that was so, why didn't Frank Indienut wait with his library visit until Christopher Bitsquirrel and Fred Bytesquirrel lifted the restriction?

"It seems to me there are only two possible explanations. Either Frank Indienut knows that dealing with the smart kernel problem will take much longer than Maggie was told, or he is so concerned about the heat storm that he feels he must monitor it. Or – both."

Gary sat down, looking exhausted.

"What a brilliant analysis!" Great-Grandpa patted Gary on his shoulder. "Unfortunately, there may be more to this scandal. And here is why.

"I have known Frank Indienut since he was a pup. In all these years, I never thought of him as a squirrel who might be involved in any kind of shady activities. In fact, I voted for him to become a council member. That's why I am wondering if Frank Indienut has been dealt a bad hand and he is trying to do the best he can.

"Maybe, he, like we, found out about the heat storm and he is monitoring it for the tribe's safety? And that's why he concocted his scheme to distract Maggie?

"Or, maybe, the entire council knows about the heat storm and told Frank to monitor it because they know that Frank's reputation is so solid that no squirrel is going to pay attention to what he is doing? And Frank is playing along because he believes it is better to monitor the storm than not.

"Anyway, I believe there are many unanswered questions. At this time, we really know only two facts: Without a doubt, some major squirrel influencers know about the heat storm, and they are trying to keep it a secret."

The room fell quiet as all squirrels seemed to ponder Great-Grandpa's thoughts. After a few minutes, Gary Logisquir got up and offered, "Let me talk to my sources."

"Who are your sources?" Great-Grandpa wanted to know.

"Two business influencers. They are not into ecommerce but they have connections," Gary replied.

Great-Grandpa nodded. Still, deep down he knew that he needed to come up with his own plan. He believed that, unfortunately, he already "waited and observed" for much too long.

34 – THE RASPBERRY EFFECT

The squirrels went home but none of them slept well.

Harry woke up in the middle of the night. Startled and worried, he went to Great-Grandpa's room but found it empty. Next, he looked into Juanita's room and saw her sleeping. Not knowing what else to do he walked to the front entrance of the burrow. Maybe Great-Grandpa had wanted to look at the stars?

"Psst, Harry."

Harry looked around but could not see anybody.

"Up here."

Squinting his eyes, Harry inspected the Big Oak. Indeed, Great-Grandpa was sitting on a second level branch. Harry dashed up the tree. "What are you doing up here?"

"I was thinking," Great-Grandpa replied. "Did you know that trees can talk?

"When trees get attacked by insects, their damaged leaves give off smells that attract birds who like to feast on these insects. In other words, the trees are asking the birds for help, in their own way.

"Trees also talk to each other using their roots. They send messages via fungi that spread along their roots. This way, plants can warn each other about droughts and other dangers. Anyway, that's why I was wondering if our trees already know about the heat storm."

"Wow. I didn't know that trees and plants could talk to each other. Hopefully, the storm is so far away that our trees don't know about it yet. What do you think of Sean, Paul, and I going on an expedition and finding out more about the heat storm?"

"Well, Harry, I think it might be wiser trying to find possible locations for building a new burrow, should it become necessary. Is this what's keeping you up?"

"No, I woke up because I dreamed of the raspberry.

"It was a nightmare. The raspberry turned into a red blob. It seems, nothing extraordinary is happening, nothing good is coming."

"Aww, Harry, you don't know that. Finding a raspberry is not like pressing a button on the smartbox and something is happening, right then. When I found my raspberries, I too did not know the significance of these finds."

"What do you mean?"

"Well, a few days after President Kennesquirrel got elected, we could not know what kind of president he would be.

"And, after I found the second raspberry, I could not know that Steve I'Squirrel's squirrelnet communicator might help save our lives. You realize without Steve's smartboxes, we wouldn't know about the heat storm. The significance of this second raspberry event proves itself even today, though Steve left us years ago. Similarly, it may take years until you know which event started on the day you found your raspberry."

"Right. I didn't think of it this way."

"Now go to bed and sleep. I'll sit here a little longer. I want to look at the moon and the stars, and my beloved trees."

35 – THE YOUNG NUTCRACKERS

Monday appeared to be a day like any other – on the surface.

Harry and Sean worked in the third potato field. But, while any passersby might have believed that the youngsters aimed to set a record of how quickly they could finish their audit, in actuality, Harry and Sean both channeled their confusion and frustrations into work. While Harry wondered what he could to do to finally launch his expedition, Sean pondered if he should advise his parents to move back to Bostonut, a burrow farther away from the heat storm than any other place he knew.

At the library, Maggie Carnegiesquir offered to get even scrolls from the top shelves "right away" though, usually, that took a wait time of at least one day. Maggie volunteered to get the scrolls right away because, secretly, she was taking inventory and calculating the number of crates needed to box up all scrolls. But the library visitors didn't know that; they thought it was their lucky day.

Quite strangely, Gary Logisquir was nowhere to be seen, all day. But while most Nuttingtonians assumed he was training with a secret sparring partner, Gary met with "his sources," on top of an 80-foot shagbark hickory, in the woods behind the lake. If any squirrel could have observed their discussion, they would have noted that all three seemed to be extremely agitated.

Meanwhile, Great-Grandpa spent all day sitting on the mighty oak tree, on a second level branch, deep in thought. A few Nuttingtonians wondered why he did not come down for lunch, though oyster mushrooms with squash salad was on the menu.

Still, the only squirrel from the Roosquirrel clan who seemed clearly in a fog was Juanita. At school, she misspelled the word Nuttington. Of course, neither Mr. Khansquirrel nor the other students could know that she felt numb, discouraged and scared. Just as she thought her life was finally good, everything she loved was threatened – again. But Mr. Khansquirrel and the other students did not know of the storm. And so, they thought Juanita just had a bad day.

The next day, Juanita seemed happier and more focused in school. It was the day of her first grassroots meeting.

The *YoungNutcrackers* met every Tuesday at the lakeside picnic area unless it rained. By the time Juanita and Harry arrived, most of the group's members were already sitting at the picnic tables. Sean was there too and waved at them. Once Juanita and Harry sat down next to Sean, Annie Speednut opened the meeting.

"Dear friends, I am delighted to welcome a new member – Juanita Squirnández. Let's give her a big round of applause and please introduce yourself."

"Hannah Martinuz, I major in Nuttology."

"Carter Wilsonut, research assistant of horticulture."

"Jacob Jonesquirrel. I am studying mathematics, but I'd rather be a singer like Johnnie Cashsquirrel."

Most *YoungNutcrackers* laughed and Carter Wilsonut hollered, "Jacob, we expect you to sing, 'Everybody Loves a Nut' later on."

"Hi Juanita." Emma Speednut waved at her. "I am majoring in smartbox technology."

"Kara Bugsquirrel, I too major in smartbox technology. My bro is a Team 2 member." Kara waved at Harry and Sean. "Paul says 'hi.' He couldn't make it today."

"Keanu Thompsquir, Deer Express messenger. I am not a student yet; I need to put aside some pistachio gold first."

"Thank you, everybody." Annie smiled and turned to Juanita. "Juanita, why don't you tell us a bit about yourself?"

Juanita, who had never attended a group meeting, looked surprised. But she collected herself quickly and said, "Hello *YoungNutcrackers*. I am Juanita Squirnández. I grew up on a barrier island close to Texas. When a huge storm hit my island and destroyed everything, a few friends and I were able to save ourselves to the mainland. Eventually, I met a few deer who worked for the Deer Express. And that's how I got here."

The *YoungNutcrackers* applauded enthusiastically.

Juanita continued. "Today was my fourth day in school. For me, this is big because on the island we did not have a school. Going to school made me realize that if we had had a school on the island, my tribe probably could have figured out how to build a boat.

"Getting educated might have saved my family. That's why I want to join the *YoungNutcrackers* . I can see why every squirrel needs an education. And – since I never owned a single pistachio gold nugget – I can also see why education needs to be affordable. Thank you for welcoming me."

The *YoungNutcrackers* cheered and gave Juanita a standing ovation.

Harry was even more impressed. He thought, "Wow, this girl is a natural. She's lived on an island, never went to a school, and she's been homeless. And yet – she can talk like that! If this tribe wants to make progress, we need her."

While the *YoungNutcrackers* awarded Juanita with the third round of applause, a squirrel walked out of the woods behind the picnic tables. Annie Speednut noticed him immediately. Always eager to welcome new members, she made a few steps toward the squirrel.

"Christopher Bitsquirrel?" she greeted the newcomer, rather surprised. "Hey there. What brings *you* here?"

"Hey, Annie. Are Harry and Sean here?" Christopher Bitsquirrel looked around nervously.

Harry and Sean who noticed him too stared at Christopher in disbelief. Of course, they could guess that Christopher Bitsquirrel's visit was about their visit to the Smartbox Center.

"Hey," Christopher greeted them. "Can I borrow you guys for a few minutes? Let's grab that picnic table over there." He pointed at a table far off.

"Sure," said Harry and thought to himself, "Stay cool! It doesn't look as if Christopher reported a break-in, or he wouldn't be here alone."

36 – CHRISTOPHER BITSQUIRREL

After they sat down, Christopher Bitsquirrel sat in silence for a minute and stared at the ground. Harry and Sean could see that he was struggling with what he wanted to say. Finally, Christopher spoke quietly, "Thank you. Thank you for helping me find the courage to come forward."

Harry and Sean didn't know how to react. They didn't know what they had done to prompt this meeting or this admission.

Still visibly nervous, Christopher continued in an incoherent way.

"I knew that I should have said something, a long time ago, but I was alone. Every time, I talked to Fred he said there is no problem… And maybe there isn't… But anyway, Fred did not want to come forward… I was alone. Then, last week, we saw you guys on the roof.

"That's when we knew that you found out… And… I am so relieved." For a brief second, Christopher smiled.

"How'd you know that we were on the roof?" Sean probed gently.

"On the roof is a camera. Kind of like a smartbox camera but different. The pictures are black and white and not very good. This camera feeds into a monitor in the storage room where we often work. Fred and I saw you guys sitting up there, under the blue panels. We don't know how you figured it out but both of us believe that you know something. Did you find out about the map?"

Harry nodded. "Yep, but it wasn't us. Mrs. Carnegiesquir did. She is the hero."

"Peanut," Christopher Bitsquirrel replied. "She can't prove how long The Council has known about this storm. But I can. Because I received Bob Smitcorn's private kuk."

Harry stared at him. "What kuk? We don't know anything about a kuk."

"It was scary. The kuk said 'This is global warming. It could destroy Nuttington." Bob also sent the URL of the site that shows the map." Christopher shuddered.

"When Fred and I saw the heat storm, we were terrified. Of course, I called a top security emergency meeting. But they did not want to do anything. "They said the kuk was not 'conclusive evidence.' They wanted to wait until we could be 100 percent certain that the heat storm is for real and that it is coming."

Christopher looked at the sky. Then, he uttered, "You know, Harry, it's not easy to become a whistleblower. Everybody is against you. You know what happened to Daniel Ellsquirrel, don't you? Fred said, if we stepped forward, The Council might blacklist us... I love my job. I don't want to lose it."

Harry patted him on the shoulder. "Calm down, calm down. You are not alone. We are with you. Now, tell me – what happened to Team 1? Did they die?"

Christopher looked befuddled. "I don't know. Until last week I always thought the entire crew died. Only when Fred and I found the faulty power kernels, I realized that this assumption might have been wrong. Maybe Bob,

Sue, and Tom are alive, stuck somewhere, without any possibility of getting in touch with us or the Deer Express."

"What's the problem with the power kernels?"

"Sorry, I forgot. So, when I received Bob's private kuk many moons ago, I reported it, but, like I said, The Council decided to wait. They are working on what they call an economic revolution. The Council thought that if the tribe members learned about the heat storm, maybe there wasn't going to be an economic revolution, or it might get delayed. They also said there was no need to worry because we could monitor the heat storm on the smartboxes.

"That's why Fred agreed not to say anything, and I was alone. Then, last week, Fred and I discovered that some of the power kernels didn't work and even Fred panicked. Sort of. Obviously, if we can't keep the smartboxes running, we can't monitor the heat storm. Of course, I immediately reported this new problem.

"The Council instructed us to check all power kernels to see how many are faulty. The big problem with that is – it's only Fred and me. The Council did not assign any extra helpers. They say they want to keep the situation 'contained.' But, if Fred and I can't get extra help, testing all kernels will take an awful lot of time."

Suddenly and unexpectedly, Christopher Bitsquirrel giggled. "But this time I was smarter. Without asking The Council I informed Bill Gatsquirrel about the power kernel problem.

"At least, that was a good move. Bill Gatsquirrel did something, right away. He immediately left for Virginia. Bill believes there is another warehouse with power kernels. Of course, we don't know if they are any good. Now The Council is waiting for Bill's report."

Looking shocked, Harry sighed audibly. "We figured out that The Council did not want anybody to know about the heat storm, but we did not know that The Council did not offer you maximum support in dealing with the power kernel problem. Want to come over to my place? Great-Grandpa will know what to do."

The three boys left without Juanita who wanted to stay at the grass-roots meeting.

37 – LEADING THE REVOLUTION

The next morning, Great-Grandpa got up early. Looking ever so serious, he made his way through the tunnels. Not too many squirrels were up at that time of the day but those who saw Great-Grandpa would tell later on that he looked all caught up in thoughts, as if pondering the Sciurus States' fate.

When he arrived at the presidential suite, Great-Grandpa told the guard that he needed to speak with the president. Now!

It turned out Great-Grandpa wasn't very much interested in what the president had to say. Of course, that was because whistle-blower Christopher Bitsquirrel had filled in the missing pieces already.

"Mr. President, as the oldest member of the tribe, I don't need to justify my interest in this pressing issue. I have lived here longer than everyone else.

"These days, I try to stay out of politics. In our family, we believe that squirrels should serve their country when they are younger. Younger squirrels tend to focus on the long-term outcomes of their enterprises.

"Which is true for the issue at hand. Nuttington's own Bob Smitcorn, Sue Millwood, and Tom Davinut demonstrated squirrelity when they warned us of a potential life-threatening danger.

"They were only kids, yet they knew what they had to do to protect the tribe.

"And what did you and The Council do? You waited, probably for your own benefit, for eighteen long months.

"Eighteen long months – which the scientists from our most excellent academies could have used to work on best solutions for all citizens.

"Most certainly, I will not stand by and watch you dishonor our youngsters' efforts and gamble with this nation's future.

"As this tribe's most senior member, I will address the tribe tonight and offer ideas. If you don't want to give me time at the burrow hall meeting, I am prepared to whistle blow all the rancid details I have learned about the kuk, the map, and the power kernel problem. Indeed, it's not a pretty picture. Good day."

After Great-Grandpa left, the president sat down in his chair which, at this moment, did not feel comfortable at all. In the back of his mind, he had always suspected that this moment would come. No secret could be kept forever. Lately, the *YoungNutcrackers* had asked too many inconvenient questions.

But The Council and he had hoped that by not addressing the student loan problem the *YoungNutcrackers* could be kept in check. Squirrel students who were buried in problems could not feel empowered as students felt during the days of President John F. Kennesquirrel's term.

What he hadn't anticipated was that a big-time influencer would lead the revolution.

38 – THE BURROW HALL MEETING

In Nuttington, burrow hall meetings were held at Nuttington Bowl. On this day, preparations were underway before the meeting started. Christopher Bitsquirrel and Fred Bytesquirrel carried a smartbox onto the stage and leaned it upright. Great-Grandpa had instructed them to record the meeting.

Squirrel citizens who showed up early were puzzled to see the unusual activity. Assuming they might get to see a live-stream video, quite a few squirrels rushed back to the burrow to get their friends who did not plan on attending the meeting.

Harry, Sean, Juanita, Maggie Carnegiesquir, and Gary Logisquir also arrived early and sat down in the second row of the coliseum. By the time the president and The Council stepped on the stage, every seat was occupied and even most of the standing room was filled — an uncommon sight at burrow hall meetings. While the government officials sat down at the back of the stage, Great-Grandpa sat down on a log piece positioned in the center of the stage.

There, he waited for Christopher's sign that the recording was working properly. Finally, he stood up, looked over the crowd, and asked in a measured tone, "Friends, Nuttingtonians, Sciuridae... Are We Nuts?"

The president's face turned ashen, and the audience gasped.

Great-Grandpa continued, "I am asking again – Are we nuts... That we do not ask questions?

"That we do not hold our leaders accountable? That we give them blank passes? That we bury the very idea of our republic?"

Great-Grandpa looked over the crowd from the right to left and back.

"We cannot pass the responsibility to act onto our leaders... Without questioning what they do."

109

Spontaneously, Annie and Emma Speednut stood up and applauded, and Jacob Jonesquirrel and Keanu Thompsquir whistled in support of Great-Grandpa's statement. Some squirrels sitting back in the bleachers stood up to get a better view of the stage.

Great-Grandpa continued, "Sadly, it turns out our leaders have secrets from us, secrets that could affect all of our lives, and our children's and childrens' children's lives.

"We might have caught them earlier...

"If we hadn't avoided asking questions.

"I myself am guilty of that.

"Though I kept observing and noticing, I stopped short of asking questions like, 'Do we know anything about this hot weather? Are you, The Council, keeping a close eye on what's happening? What measures are you taking to ensure the safety of the squirrel nation?'"

He paused to give his audience an opportunity to let the questions sink in.

Then, he continued, "Generations ago, the Founding Squirrels recognized that – together – we squirrels are stronger. And right they were."

With a sweeping gesture, Great-Grandpa pointed at Nuttington Bowl, the beach, and the burrow behind the seating area.

"Look what we have accomplished. We built all of this – with our own paws! No other species has come close to dominating our region like we have.

"And, yet – if we don't live by the principles of squirrelity, we risk it all. And – if too many of our leaders don't stick to the principles of squirrelity, life in the Sciurus States may get stale or rancid.

"Last week, some of my friends and I noted efforts of our leaders to keep it a secret that life in the Sciurus States may be threatened – a huge heat storm is looming southwest of the Sciurus States."

The audience gasped nervously. Murmuring could be heard from every corner of the auditorium, not only from the back. Great-Grandpa motioned with his arms for the crowd to quiet down.

"You know what this means. All of us could die. The air might get so hot that most of us die from heat stroke and the rest of us might starve to death. Because there won't be enough food. The heat will cause algae to bloom in the ponds and lakes. Hence, we might not even have anything to drink."

Great-Grandpa turned around and looked at the council members. Then, he said solemnly, "No economic revolution is worth risking our lives because we won't be able to enjoy our success.

"We don't know if and where the heat storm will strike but *this* is the moment to act. In fact, we have already lost eighteen months.

"Nuttington's excellent and dedicated Team 1 discovered the heat storm and reported it. Bob Smitcorn, Sue Millwood, and Tom Davinut may even have risked their lives to warn us. We have not heard from these heroes since.

"We owe it to them, our ancestors, and our children and unborn children to move forward and save the republic. Over the coming weeks and months, each of us will have to contribute in our own best ways. Luckily, squirrels are born doers. It's squirrels' temperament to work hard and to work smart. And – we will!"

The audience rose to their feet and applauded.

Great-Grandpa waited for a minute and then continued, "The very idea of our republic is *not* that we elect leaders and don't question their actions.

"That's what we had when man was king of the land. Then, we squirrels could not question King Man's actions. In our republic we can, and we must.

"In the words of founding squirrel Thomas Jeffersquirrel, 'Whenever the squirrels are well-informed, they can be trusted with their own government.'"

Great-Grandpa glanced again at the council members and the president. Then, he ended his speech by saying, "And, one more thing.

"On our journey to finding the truth, we learned that at least one squirrel citizen was afraid to speak up about the wrongs he saw.

"This is a free nation. In the Sciurus States, no squirrel should be afraid to speak up and share discriminating information. To avoid that this is happening again, we need to establish an anonymous hotline.

"My great-grandson Harry and Christopher Bitsquirrel tell me that squirrels who might be afraid to reveal what's wrong in their burrows can open an anonymous account on the *Smart Kuks&Quaas.*

"They also tell me that kuks posted from an anonymous account can be found if the anonymous tipster adds a hashtag. So, we created a hashtag for all squirrels who want to question something or reveal problems at their burrows.

"That hashtag is #AreWeNuts.

"Christopher Bitsquirrel, Maggie Carnegiesquir, and I hereby invite you to use it.

Thank you."

While the president's and the council members' mouths dropped open, the audience rose to their feet and started clapping wildly. And Annie Speednut led a chorus of *YoungNutcrackers* who chanted "ARE... WE ... NUTS... ARE... WE... NUTS."

After that went on for a good while, Harry smiled, turned to Juanita, and said, "It's the raspberry event."

"Huh?"

"I'll tell you later, during dinner."

39 – THE KUK-REVOLUTION

The next day, in the late afternoon, Great-Grandpa headed to the library. Maggie Carnegiesquir greeted him with a warm smile.

"Good afternoon, Archibald, I am so happy to see you. What a night it was, yesterday. I am so proud of you."

Great-Grandpa sat down on a comfy straw bag chair and briefly closed his eyes. After a minute or so, he said, "Good afternoon, Maggie. My apologies for being so emotional. Indeed, it is absolutely stupendous what happened since yesterday.

"This morning, Harry, Sean, and Paul started preparing for their expedition. Juanita will accompany them to the next large burrow to form a new chapter of the *YoungNutcrackers* there. Gary Logisquir decided not to defend his title at the National Nut-Checkers Championship in Shenandoah and instead run for office. Also, Harry told me that the academy's smartbox technology students are all at the Smartbox Center, testing power kernels. And Christopher received a kuk from Bill Gatsquirrel that he is now getting help from local students, up there, in Virginia.

"Most importantly, Christopher made contact with Athenburrow academy's scientists, at the Sciurus States' most southwestern academy. Of course, that region is most threatened by the heat storm. Christopher sent them the URL of the weather site so they are warned."

"And that's only what happened till lunch time. I haven't seen any of the kids since then. I was busy helping Gary design his election posters."

Quiet talk could be heard from the media room next door. Great-Grandpa looked startled. "Am I interrupting?"

Maggie shook her head. "No, no, you are not interrupting anything." She put her index finger over her lips and motioned for him to get up. Then, Maggie took him by the paw and led him to the entrance of the media room. Peeking inside, Great-Grandpa's chin dropped.

On the floor, Harry, Juanita, Annie Speednut, and Christopher Bitsquirrel were huddled around one of the smartboxes. They were busy reading kuks & quaas.

"Another kuk about wildfires in Georgia," Harry said.

Annie Speednut made a checkmark on a scroll. "That brings up the number of wildfire incidences to twenty-eight," she said.

Maggie pulled Great-Grandpa back into the main room. "They have been here since noon," she whispered. "They are evaluating the results of the #AreWeNuts hashtag campaign."

Great-Grandpa exhaled. "Holy pistachio. Maggie, please enlighten this technology-challenged squirrel, would you?"

Maggie laughed quietly. "With your speech you stirred up squirrels all over the Sciurus States. This morning, Christopher Bitsquirrel trimmed the last piece of your speech out of the video, the one about the hashtag. He put it on the *Smart Kuks&Quaas.*

"Since then, over five hundred kuks with the hashtag #AreWeNuts have been posted. When Christopher saw this, he told Harry. The kids came here to read the kuks. At times, librarians all over the country had to shut down their smartboxes because so many squirrels wanted to extend their thanks, send their congrats, and post questions they felt needed to be asked. It appears *you* started the Kuk Revolution."

"Holy Pistachio," uttered Great-Grandpa. Looking stunned, he scratched his ears and then asked, "Maggie, would you consider taking a brief break from watching this Kuk Revolution?

"I actually came here because I wanted to ask you if you are nuts enough to watch the sunset at the beach – with me? I saw wispy high clouds out there. If we hurry up, we might be able to see a gorgeous sunset."

"Archibald, this is a lovely idea. It's past library hours anyway."

At the beach, Great-Grandpa and Maggie Carnegiesquir sat down on a bench. Great-Grandpa put his arm around Maggie's shoulder and said, "Look, the sky is almost the color of raspberries."

Maggie nodded. "Like magic," she said and leaned her head against his shoulder.

Neither one of them saw Harry who stood at the back entrance of the burrow, watching them with a happy grin.

Harry too marveled at the sky. "The future is uncertain," he thought. "Maybe Nuttington burrow won't survive. But look how far we have come already, in such a short time."

Then, he returned to the library to work some more.

Let us put our minds together
and see what life we can make for our children.
– Sitting Bull

BOOK CLUB QUESTIONS

1. Fables are meant to be didactic lessons given through some sort of animal story. Do you think the author succeeded in this endeavor?

2. Who is your favorite squirrel character? Why?

3. What was your favorite part of "Are We Nuts?"?

4. What was your least favorite?

5. What aspects of "Are We Nuts?" could you most relate to?

6. Are all or most major themes of "Are We Nuts" relevant in your life?

7. How well do you think the author built the world of squirrels, the Sciurus States?

8. "Are We Nuts?" mentions more than two dozen famous Sciuridae (Sciurus States' squirrels) whose names and work remind of famous Americans. They include 6 presidents/founder squirrels, 8 entrepreneurs/business influencers (living and dead)), 5 explorers/scientists and 6 artists/athletes. How many did you discover?

9. Share a favorite quote from "Are We Nuts?". Why did it stand out for you?

10. What surprised you most about "Are We Nuts?"?

11. What other fables have you read?

12. Were you glad you read "Are We Nuts?"? Would you recommend it to a friend?

13. Who do you most want to read this book?

STUDENT QUESTIONS

15 Questions for students (History/ Civics/ Government/ Science/ Business):

1. Which elements of the squirrels' story sounded familiar to you?

2. Which "squirrel greats" reminded you of famous people, living or deceased?

3. In the story, which inventions and best practices helped the squirrels in becoming a more successful society?

4. What are some of the problems Nuttington's residents experience?

5. What problems do the squirrel society experience to which you see parallels in our society?

6. Imagine you are one of the Founding Fathers of the Sciurus States. Come up with five policies you would create to ensure the survival of the Nuttington tribe and the squirrel nation.

7. Why was Juanita worried if she could succeed in the squirrel republic? What problems might you encounter if you moved to a different city, state, or country?

8. Is it better for the squirrels to live on trees or in burrows? What are the advantages and disadvantages? (Keep in mind the squirrel's harvest-to-storage processes, their need to protect themselves from different kinds of predators, their wish to live an ambitious live style as well as potential environmental problems.)

9. If you were Nuttington's city planner, how would you design the burrow?

10. Are the Sciurus States a land of opportunity?

11. What do you think of Christopher Bitsquirrel's way to handle his complicated situation?

12. Why does The Squirrel Council keep the information about the heat storm a secret? Do you know of parallels in our world?

13. What do you think of Great-Grandpa's speech at the burrow hall meeting?

14. What should be the goal of Harry's/Team 2's expedition:

    a) investigate the heat storm,

    b) find a better suited location for a new burrow (within the 13 states of the republic or elsewhere)

    c) something else

15. In the story, all main characters take action once they discover the looming climate disaster. What do you think do individual Americans, companies, influencers, and governments need to do to avoid a climate disaster on planet Earth?

12 more involved questions for students

1. "Are We Nuts?" mentions more than two dozen famous Sciuridae (Sciurus States' squirrels) whose names and work reminds of famous Americans. They include 6 presidents/founder squirrels, 8 entrepreneurs/business influencers (living and dead)), 5 explorers/scientists and 6 artists/athletes. How many did you discover?

2. "Are We Nuts?" mentions a total of 8 famous phrases/quotes, 4 of which featured in books, plays, or movies, 3 said by presidents (an inaugural address, a farewell speech, and a speech given at the Sorbonne), and 1 said by a famous explorer. How many did you discover?

3. Did you discover similarities between the development of the United States and that of the Sciurus States? What are they?

4. What is the cornerstone of the Sciurus States' success? Does the same concept work for the U.S. businesses/the economy too?

5. How should governments balance the rights of individuals with the common good?

6. Did squirrel president Theo Roosquirrel's "Square Deal for Squirrels" remind you of U.S. president Theodore Roosevelt's "Square Deal"? Can you describe Roosevelt's "Square Deal"?

7. Imagine you are a squirrel entrepreneur in the Sciurus States. What new product would you invent? If possible, provide sketches or technical drawings.

8. Why was Juanita worried whether she could succeed in the squirrel republic? Do you believe that young Americans experience similar issues?

9. What do you think are Juanita's goals as she sets out to form a new chapter of the *YoungNutcrackers* at a burrow where she has never lived? How should she go about it?

10. What office will Gary Logisquir be running for? What principles, goals, and positions on domestic affairs will he support? Why do you think that?

11. Write Gary Logisquir's announcement to run for office and design his campaign poster.

Thank you for reading my fable "Are We Nuts?"

Are you wondering why I decided featuring squirrels as the story's protagonists?

Squirrels are extremely intelligent. Some say they are the 9ᵗʰ most intelligent animals, surprisingly similar to primates. Squirrels assess nuts by turning them in their paws. Doing this helps them in determining the shapes and weights of nuts as well as spotting holes or cracks in their shells.

If squirrels believe that they are being watched by other squirrels or birds, they will fake bury loot and store them somewhere else safely. They also don't hide their loot "just about anywhere" but use "spatial chunking." The technique could be compared to how people store foods in pantries – squirrels bury different kinds of nuts in different geographical areas.

Squirrels use their own "language" of kuks and quaas, moans, and mukmuks to warn others. They "adopt" orphaned pups if the babies are related to the adoptive mother.

The International Union for Conservation of Nature registered the squirrel on its list of the top 100 invasive species which is largely attributed to that fact that squirrels learn and keep learning by observing others. Squirrels live in almost every habitat excluding the high polar regions and the driest of deserts. They also do well living in cities.

The clever animal is the Native American symbol for preparation, trust, and thriftiness.

If you like my fable, please post a review and share your thoughts.

I hope you will find a reason to give "Are We Nuts" as a gift to family members and friends, especially young people.

Gisela Hausmann

ABOUT THE AUTHOR

Gisela Hausmann is a multi award-winning author, email evangelist and speaker.

Her work has been featured on Bloomberg and Geekwire (tech podcasts), in *SUCCESS, Entrepreneur, and Inc.*

Born to be an adventurer, Gisela has co-piloted single-engine planes, produced movies, and worked in the industries of education, construction, and international transportation. Gisela's friends and fans know her as a woman who goes out to seek the unusual and rare adventure.

A unique mixture of wild risk-taker and careful planner, Gisela globe-trotted almost 100,000 kilometers on three continents, including to the locations of her favorite books: Doctor Zhivago's Russia, Heinrich Harrer's Tibet, and Genghis Khan's Mongolia.

These days, Gisela is an active environmentalist who runs the air condition as little as possible, dries her laundry on a clothesline, mows the lawn in sections so there is always enough clover for bees to feast on, and doesn't use weedkillers or other harsh chemicals. She also planted 38 trees (so far).

Gisela Hausmann graduated with a master's degree in Film & Mass Media from the University of Vienna. She now lives in Greenville, South Carolina.

Gisela's website: http://www.giselahausmann.com/

Follow her at https://twitter.com/Naked_Determina

OTHER BOOKS BY GISELA HAUSMANN

Naked Determination, 41 Stories About Overcoming Fear
Naked Eye-Opener: To Reach the Dream You Must Forget About It
Inside Amazon: My Story

NAKED WORDS 2.0: The Effective 157-Word Email
NAKED TEXT Email Writing Skills for Teenagers
73 Ways to Turn a Me-Mail Into an E-mail
BAT SHIT CRAZY Review Requests: Email Humor

The Little Blue Book for Authors:
- 53 Dos & Don'ts Nobody Is Telling You
- 101 Clues to Get More Out of Facebook
- Essential Manners for the Modern Author

NAKED TRUTHS About Getting Book Reviews 2018
Naked Good Reads: How to find Readers
BOOK MARKETING: The Funnel Factor: Including 100 Media Pitches
Naked News for Indie Authors: How NOT to Invest Your Marketing $$$

NAKED TRUTHS About Getting Product Reviews on Amazon.com: 7
Insider tips to boost Sales
Die NACKTE WAHRHEIT ÜBER PRODUKT REZENSIONEN auf
Amazon.com: Insider enthüllt 7 Tipps für mehr Umsatz (German Edition)

http://www.giselahausmann.com/books.html

COPYRIGHT ATTRIBUTIONS

Cover:
Black and white engrave isolated squirrel illustration: Evgeny Turaev / Shutterstock
Document about America's independence Zakharova_Elenay Zakharova_Elena / Shutterstock
Old paper scroll by Andrey_Kuzmin / Shutterstock
Heap of mixed nuts by Studio Mars / Shutterstock
Map of the Thirteen Original Colonies: This media file is in the public domain in the United States. This applies to U.S. works where the copyright has expired, often because its first publication occurred prior to January 1, 1923. - Attribution: Centpacrr at English Wikipedia

Squirrels:
[Harry] Grey squirrel by Meister 199 / Pixabay
[Juanita] Black squirrel by Rostislav Kralik / Shutterstock
[smartbox technician] Squirrel by Eric Isselee / Shutterstock
[Great-Grandpa] Grey squirrel by J A Uppendahl / Shutterstock
[Gary Logisquir] White squirrel by Tony Campbell / Shutterstock
[Sean O'Squirrel] Red squirrel by NadiaTighe / Pixabay
[Maggie Carnegiesquir] Red squirrel by Geert Weggen / Shutterstock
[Steve Lobbynut] Chipmunk by Mandy Cherundolo / Shutterstock
[Dick Hushsquirrel] Golden-mantled ground squirrel by Nina B / Shutterstock
[Cee-Kee Allsquirrel] Southern flying squirrel by Tony Campbell / Shutterstock
[Annie & Emma] Squirrel isolated by Dark_Side / Shutterstock
[Harry inside the duct] Gray squirrel by IrinaK / Shutterstock
[Christopher Bitsquirrel] Gray squirrel by Svetlana Foote / Shutterstock

Other viuals:

Wooden Frame by guruXOX / Shutterstock
Sackcloth by SeDmi / Shutterstock
Wooden Mobile Stand gd_project / Shutterstock
Seeds and nuts with collection by Pakhnyushchy / Shutterstock
Abstract art by Natalia Penado / Shutterstock
Black Smartphone by Denis Semenchenko / Shutterstock
Topographical map of the United States of America by www.demis.nl
Dust sand cloud by Evgenia Vasileva / Shutterstock
Galvanized steel air duct by Denis Torkhov / Shutterstock
Bar chart graph by jongcreative / Shutterstock